The Tree
& other stories

by Abdallah al-Nasser
translated by Dina Bosio and Christopher Tingley

with an introduction by Salma Khadra Jayyusi

Interlink Books

An imprint of Interlink Publishing Group, Inc.
Northampton, Massachusetts

First published in 2004 by

INTERLINK BOOKS
An imprint of Interlink Publishing Group, Inc.
46 Crosby Street, Northampton, Massachusetts 01060
www.interlinkbooks.com

Copyright © Abdallah al-Nasser 2004
Translation copyright © Salma Khadra Jayyusi 2004

All rights reserved. No part of this publication may be reproduced, stored in a retrieval system, or transmitted in any form or by any means, electronic, mechanical, photocopying, recording or otherwise without the prior permission of the publisher.

Library of Congress Cataloging-in-Publication Data
Naasir, Abd Allaah Mohammad.
[Short stories. English. Selections]
The tree and other stories / by Abdallah al-Nasser ; translated by Dina Bosio and Christopher Tingley.—1st American ed.
p. cm.—(Interlink world fiction)
ISBN 1-56656-498-0
1. Short stories, Arabic—Saudi Arabia—Translations into English.
2. Arabic fiction—20th century—Translations into English.
I. Title. II. Series.
PJ8005.82.E5N372 2003
892.7'3010806—dc22
2003016465

This English translation is published with the cooperation of PROTA (the Project of Translation from Arabic); director: Salma Khadra Jayyusi, Cambridge, Massachusetts, USA

Cover painting "Blue Paradise," 1989, by Suad Attar, courtesy of The Royal Society of Fine Arts, Jordan National Gallery of Fine Art, Amman, Jordan

Printed and bound in Canada by Webcom

To request our complete 40-page full-color catalog, please call us toll free at **1-800-238-LINK,** visit our website at **www.interlinkbooks.com,** or write to
Interlink Publishing
46 Crosby Street, Northampton, MA 01060
e-mail: info@interlinkbooks.com

Contents

Introduction vii

The Tree 1
Abu Rashed 7
The Bird of Fury 13
The Composition Lesson 17
The Mirage 25
Redemption 30
Shabash! 34
The Tunnel 38
The Novel 44
The Family Home 48
Mohaymeed 54
At the Company of Hope 59
Sabeh al-Layl 69
Editor-in-Chief 73
Hassan's Theory 78
The Cat 84
The Tin Can 86
Setting Out 88
The Committee 92
Tears in the Darkness 96
Flocks of Doves 102
The Snow Siege 107
Um Rajoum 114

Notes 123

Introduction

Abdallah al-Nasser is one of those authors who tends to write the short story according to its preliminary requirements: that is to say, as a compact account of a limited event, with no intention of extending the bounds of time or flowing beyond the initial purpose of recounting an incident or a single experience. There are many short story writers who cover, within a single story, an extended span of the protagonist's life. Here in al-Nasser's stories, the single event or experience remains the focus.

The short narrative in classical Arabic, often expressed in the *khabar* form, usually claimed factuality. This was due to abhorrence, at the advent of Islam, of the wayward imagination commonly qualifying fictional writings in pre-Islamic times, as found in such works as the *Book of Crowns* (*kitab al-tijan*). Islam insisted on literal truth, and this tended to curb the imagination and stop its soaring to unlimited heights. The *khabar* genre, which almost always began with a chronological account of transmitters, guaranteed at least the semblance of truth. As with countless narrative accounts in this classical tradition, al-Nasser writes episodically – in a fashion, that is to say, as old as the earliest Arabic writings and as new as the present-day Arab renaissance, which has launched fiction into the modern world. Still alive, today, is the memory of those thousands of anecdotal episodes that filled so many books and compendiums in the old culture, covering, piecemeal, the whole infinitely varied panorama of Arabic life in medieval time.

Abdallah al-Nasser is well versed in classical Arabic literature; and the riches of the traditional anecdote, which is often in effect a short story, have exerted an influence on him as on so many other writers. Numerous Classical Arabic books—such as *Al-Aghani* (the Book of Songs), M. al-Tanukhi's *Table Talk of a Mesopotamian Judge* (*nishwar al-muhadara*), in eight volumes, and his equally famous but smaller book, *Reprieve after Hardship* (*al-faraj ba'da 'l-shidda*), and many others—were composed of such anecdotes, and the modern Arab writer venturing on the short story in modern times must necessarily have inherited his ancestors' gaze on the world, seeing it not in terms of broad and continuous flow, not as a totality of life wherein the protagonists' destiny is seen (as Lukacs would put it), against an entire world proceeding through time but in its particular experience: moments of joy, or stress, or contemplation; single acts of generosity, hospitality, revenge, loyalty, cruelty, magnanimity, wisdom, open and suppressed sexuality, ardor, sensuality, asceticism, all the experiences medieval Arabs knew. These ranged from desert life with its limited yet paradoxically universal experience, its dire deprivation of the luxuries enjoyed in the adjacent civilizations of Persia and Byzantium, and its persistent struggle for survival, to the city life of Arabs of the urban centuries, with its multiracial and highly colorful public, its licentious experiences, its awe of authority, its pomp, luxury, power, and money, its periodic adventure outside the limits of space and tradition, its yearning for wealth with the rise of an early middle class in Baghdad and other metropolitan centers. The Classical Arabic anecdote, a short story par excellence, is ingrained in the consciousness of modern Arabs in touch with their heritage.

Al-Nasser is writing in an age of robust literary activity that has involved the whole Arab world from the Gulf to the Atlantic. It is an age during which the Arab creative impulse has remained unstopped by national catastrophes; there has rather been a major effervescence of literary output, some in new areas of creativity, following some of the most harrowing man-made disasters that can threaten a people and its culture. These disasters were twofold. The first were imposed by the external enemy, primarily Israel and neo-colonialism, and stemmed from the colossal aggressions to which the Arab world was subjected: the 1948 Palestine disaster, the 1956 tripartite attack on Egypt, the 1967 June War, and the constant atrocity practiced by Israel against the Palestinians and other Arabs. This produced a frank and open literature, filled with loudly voiced protest and, at times, with rhetorical overtones. The second disaster stemmed from internal aggression, which, at its worst, subjected the Arab citizen to constant humiliation and deprivation of rights, and, if he showed dissent and expressed open criticism, terrorized him at least with deprivation of his livelihood and often with penalties threatening his very life. This situation produced obliquity in literature: allusions, symbols, and a major venture into difficult imagery whose significance might escape the censor's eye. The Arab people are now, still, on the receiving end of internal governmental repression while, at the same time, suffering persistent external aggression, instability and a constant hunt for solutions. Yet all this, far from curbing the wish to create, seems to have deepened the will to assert the life of the mind and the creative imagination.

Arab writers have demonstrated a vigilant, multi-colored creativity, a competitive search for new ways of expression and a brisk experimentation in new forms. The novel's incorporation into Arabic as a genre of major importance took place in the mid-20th century. Drama also took a concerted turn, with serious attempts at dramatic writing taking place in all parts of the Arab world, including the Gulf region. Meanwhile, the short story itself, already established during the first half of the twentieth century, continued to flourish; and poetry, the Arabs' oldest and most respected art, underwent, at the same time, the greatest technical revolution in its long history. Moreover, the resurgence in the national literatures of the Arab world has spread beyond the Arab heartland (Egypt, Lebanon, Syria, Palestine, Jordan, and Iraq, where an established tradition of literary activity had existed since the Arab literary renaissance of the nineteenth century) to engage young writers all over the Arab world. In the Gulf region, literature, in its modern forms, was still generally inactive in the first half of the twentieth century. It is true, having said that, that the parts now covered by Saudi Arabia had always enjoyed a degree of special status, and a divergent cultural history, vis-à-vis the rest of the Arab Peninsula. Following its centrality during the early centuries of Islam (particularly in Hijaz, with its holy cities of Mecca and Medina) this region remained the custodian of specific literary traditions, preserving them with pride and maintaining them faithfully in their old garb. Because the region was the early seat of the religion, a profound conservatism, both social and literary, developed. This had a double edge: it conserved, with tenacity, much of what was good in

INTRODUCTION

the old linguistic and literary traditions, but it eventually posed a major obstacle to the modern Saudi writer striving to enter the vast, colorful, and highly innovative domain of modern Arabic literature. This is why the successful emergence of writers like Abdallah al-Nasser and a number of others of his generation, is something to admire; for these writers, in their quest for modernity and contemporaneity with their colleagues in the Arab heartland, had to transcend far more than did the other peninsular Arabs (tiny Bahrain was the first to demonstrate an interest in literary modernity): a rooted, settled outlook and an established tradition of literary expression, viewed as infallible and governed from a conservative standpoint infiltrated by pietisms and entrenched classicism.

Abdallah al-Nasser has lived a number of years in the West, three in the United States and more than ten in London. His outlook on the "other" stems from an achieved harmony that has merged notions from both cultures, while remaining fundamentally true to his own culture and to its finest expressions of aesthetic and humane tradition: the spontaneous generosity, the enthusiasm and loyalty for all that was pure and noble in the old Arab life, for Arab-Islamic civilization, for the glory of past achievements, and, above all, for the old poetic and literary traditions and the whole vista of Arab-Islamic history. No matter how well attuned to a life in the West, Abdallah al-Nasser maintains the full integrity of his inherited culture, a rooted Arabic heritage over fifteen centuries old. In the light of this heritage, he can only see the "other" as revolving within a different orbit, with a different cultural concept of life and human interaction, some of which he, according to inherited Islamic norms, treats with liberal acceptance. This is clearly seen in his story

"The Snow Siege," where the anguish of a Western woman unable to make a necessary journey due to lack of funds stirs in the old Arab protagonist his chivalry toward women, and his irrepressible urge to give where help is needed. This cultural seal of ethical deportment is a perfect representation of inherited Arab norms, enacted in a distinctly different culture where the differentness is not a variable but an opposing stance. Such works of fiction furnish a mine of information for the study of cultural differences in a world now seeking to impose a one-sided view of human culture and behavior.

There are, nevertheless, certain instances where al-Nasser finds himself unable to tolerate what he views as basic divergences from inherited Arab ethics in some Western culture. We see this in his story "The Family Home," where he engages an image of what he believes to be the presence of detached father-son relationships in British culture. He is here describing an extreme situation of alienation and irresponsibility, where a son, for monetary reasons, evicts his father from his home, condemning him to live in poverty and loneliness away from his grandchildren. Such unusual cases, if they existed, would always be profoundly shocking to those reared within an Arabic culture, particularly a traditional culture like that of Saudi Arabia, where a father is customarily honored, and where, according to Islamic law, the son is legally obliged to provide for his parents when they are poor. It is interesting also to see how al-Nasser subtly introduces the family dog as needing greater care and hence a greater income, adding another reason for the financial necessity of evicting the father. This entails the sharpest possible edge of irony, here left implicit, vis-à-vis Arab-Islamic values. The acceptance of Western attitudes manifested in "The Snow Siege" is absent

Introduction

here, in connection with what he feels to be Western norms in family relationships. For all that, the story is technically balanced and is not marred by sentimentality or a resort to preaching and direct criticism. The plot is well developed, and the full implications of the story revealed only at the very end.

Al-Nasser exhibits a varied experience and a frequent, powerful gift of insight. The diversity in his collections is wide and colorful, the variety—not just of themes but also of approaches—unusually rich. He is sometimes sardonic without being cynical, sarcastic without being harsh, sometimes light-heartedly humorous, particularly at people's simple-minded ignorance and naïveté. Yet he is always a sharp observer of the human condition in its widely variable aspect; and, while he can be completely down to earth and realistic, he can also sometimes soar delightfully into the realms of fantasy. Although al-Nasser is true to his vocation as a short story writer, in that he concentrates more on the depiction of situations than on development and analysis of character, he does sometimes, through the delineation of a particular situation, provide a clear profile of the main protagonist. This is seen in his story "Tears in the Darkness," where a once successful and affluent businessman, now reduced to utter penury, suffers the anguish of remembered mistakes, self-flagellation, and bitter regret. In a story of this kind we actually begin, in a sense, at the end point, with no portrayal of the details—the actual history of a failed career—that has led to this point. Such short stories are at times found in modern Arabic. Many of his short stories, as said above, remain loyal to the old notion, whereby brief narration of a single event culminates in an unforeseen ending. A notable example of this is his story "The Wolf" (in the Project for the Translation of

Arabic's *Anthology of Modern Arabic Fiction* from Columbia University Press). Held up before us is a mirror to an episode in human life, where a problem is posed or a significant issue raised, and a resolution finally achieved.

Yet al-Nasser is capable, too, of flouting all these rules and producing a multi-dimensional short narrative laden with symbolization and allusion, and pointing to a much broader, far more profound human experience. This is well represented in the splendid title story "The Tree," which has been described to me by a highly experienced reader as one of the most striking short stories he has encountered anywhere in modern Arabic writing. Here, in a remarkably short space, we find a finished treatment of the struggle between modernity and tradition, change and permanence, adventure and resistance, which not just the oil-rich Gulf countries but the old world everywhere have experienced. Moving, illuminating, and precise, it summarizes the tragic necessity of modernity and the futility of attempting to combat the winds of change. In this story al-Nasser exploits the genre in a different, more modern and inclusive fashion, single-mindedly bent, indeed, on a single experience, but here a communal experience.

There is in al-Nasser's stories a fundamental nostalgia, found in a number of writers in the Gulf region, for a world vanishing beneath their eyes with the advent of oil, money and modernization. (See also the work of Abd al-Hameed Ahmad, from the United Arab Emirates, with such stories as "The Palm Tree Said to the Sea…" and "Khlalah SEL" and Abdallah Ali Khalifa of Bahrain, with his "The Bird," in my anthology, *The Literature of Modern Arabia*.) This aspiration toward a bygone life and its irrecoverable innocence also carries with it, in part at least, a kind of futile rejection of new attitudes brought about by modernization and affluence. The old innocence and the trusty way of life are here elegized, with skill and great decorum. Yet finally the writer, for all his pull toward a vanishing world, does not reject the possibility, even the necessity of change. Deep within him is an instinctive rejection of hybridity and an abrupt, unselective Westernization, but he will, in the end, acquiesce in the inevitable that the radical change of material circumstances has imposed. Such a change has characterized the new life throughout this region, though laying the greatest burden of all on Saudi Arabia, which is *de facto* guardian of Islamic and Arab norms inherited from time immemorial, and the cradle of two of the holiest Islamic shrines of Mecca and Medina (the third, of course, being Jerusalem).

Al-Nasser is, then, questioning destiny, nursing a clouded, indeed impossible dream that neither he nor his imagined protagonists can achieve or even truly wish to achieve. The hands of the clock will not be turned back. Life has entered a different time zone, and a different zone of space. Not just in "The Tree" but in other stories too, the author shows an awareness that the vision of innocence, of a simple, well-protected life will continue to recede until it vanishes at last, leaving behind only a memory of something settled and anchored that could find no place in this new life opening out on myriad necessary (and at times unnecessary) possibilities.

Because history has set them as guardians over Islam's most sacred sites, the Saudis have had a special and unique experience in striving to preserve the dignity of this trust, and the eternal, gratifying bond it entails. They grapple, and will continue to grapple, with the forces threatening to change an inherited and established way of life: to struggle to keep what must perforce disappear, to protect what the winds of change are bound to rend asunder. This will be a source of great pain for the Saudis, who will bear the brunt of modernity's difficult birth, its unrelenting pressures, its vertiginous pull and harsh, unavoidable adventure, its inharmonious but irrevocable surge in their lives.

Among other characteristics of al-Nasser's work is an invincible faith in survival; this is seen in much of his work, opening the way to optimism and to trust in ultimate deliverance. A spirit of resistance prevails in such stories as "The Bird of Fury." Also found, however, is gratuitous deliverance, viewed as part of the law of living and continuity. This last governs his story "Um Rajoum" about people lost and then saved in the desert. In fact, his desert stories are some of the most moving in his work, introducing images of experience salvaged from memory or hearsay, making the reader more fully aware of the dangers that besiege man on earth, of the vulnerability and fragility of life. In these desert stories, the Arab reader is all at once placed in touch with his ancestors, with an experience more than 2,000 years old, when the Arab braved the desert in quest of water, pasture, and survival, and suffered throughout his existence the desert's treacherous assault and forbidding dangers. Interestingly, al-Nasser shows how the desert still, in modern times, has the capacity to swallow and destroy. In one of his stories, he has the car take the place of the eternal camel that straddled the expanse of the wilderness for centuries on end. Finally, the camel becomes the only means of saving the driver bogged down in the sand, his vehicle now totally destroyed by the desert elements. It is a major act of homage to the animal whose history is inexorably linked to the history of the Arab people and their literature, to a memory that the old Arabic poetry will forever preserve. It takes, nonetheless, a deeply perceptive writer from Saudi Arabia to bring all this back to life with dignity and love, humanizing our alienation, in an age of technology, from the desert and its tenacious beast.

And yet there is another side to this writer so skilled in elegizing a lost time; and that is his capacity to see the comic side of experience, and of human behavior generally. Returning to "The Wolf," we find here a paradoxical inversion of experience, ending in a comic portrayal of human frailty and the human capacity for self-delusion. A family's fear of a stray wolf in the neighborhood sets its members on watch, resolved to surprise and kill this predator and so live in peace. As they watch through the dark, their quarry comes into view at last, and one of them manages to kill it. Thereupon they all sleep in peace, only to find out next morning that they have merely killed the family donkey. Such an inversion of the expected is found in the heightened tragi-comic resolution of stories by other Gulf writers, as in the outstanding "Khlalah SEL" by Abd al-Hameed Ahmad, mentioned earlier. The ignorant newly rich Bedouin Khlalah, who in pre-oil times had been a water seller, carrying water to people's homes on his cherished donkey, has now, through land purchase and distribution by the new oil government, built a house and acquired a Mercedes and driver. The once priceless, irreplaceable donkey is found dead and rotting between the walls of Khlalah's and the neighbors' new houses, having squeezed himself in there, unmissed until the stench finally drew people's notice; an ironic twist, and a telling comment on the riches come to a once desolate world.

A fundamentally realistic writer, al-Nasser still shows recognition of certain old concepts, especially parental authority. There is no hostility in his work toward the father figure, whose authority, usually a mixture of ruthless hegemony and tender affection, was early contested by such heartland writers as the Lebanese Laila Baalbaki, in her seminal first novel, *I Live* (1958). It is also very interesting to note that there is, in Gulf creative literature generally, very little political self-criticism. This stands in contrast to the powerful critique of governments, of autocratic rulers, and of the staid continuity of outmoded concepts and cultural norms, that is widespread in the rest of the Arab world, albeit commonly offered through symbolization or allusion. The basic issues in Gulf literature seem to lie elsewhere: in the daily interactions of individuals now at variance in attitudes and sensibilities, in the way they face modernization and change of circumstances, in the psychological effect of sudden wealth, in the move from Bedouin desert life to that of the city, in the difficulty of parting with old attachments and entrenched habits and ways of behavior; and, very often, in the swiftly vanishing face of trust and innocence.

For all his firm classical roots, al-Nasser uses the modernized Arabic language employed in much of contemporary Arabic literature. He does not strive to discover a complex literary style liable to halt the flow of ideas and images by drawing attention to its own linguistic and rhetorical allure. In a usually relaxed style, he writes a prose admirably direct and free of rhetorical devices, with artifice almost completely absent. He has no patience with linguistic exertion. Rather, there is a depth of insight in much of his work, an ardent engagement with the problems of life in a rapidly changing world. All this helps enlarge our sympathies and deepen our understanding of the real-life issues of Arabia and its people.

—Salma Khadra Jayyusi

The Tree

It was an old, pale tree, older than anyone could remember—as old, you might have thought—as the hills and rocks surrounding it. Its roots went deep into the earth, tangled in all directions, and they were as strong as iron.

The tree's story was like the land's, in all its roughness. The trunk, strong and hollowed out, was used by travellers and wayfarers as a chimney for the fires they lit, leaving ashes and charred logs behind them. The people regarded this tree as their own heritage; and, since it stood to the northern side of the village, they actually called the north the "tree side." They'd gather under the tree, too, whenever they held a meeting or before embarking on a trip. The village council was always held beneath it and decisions taken there. Then, it was the place where they took their naps along with their animals. Even the rain was measured using the trunk, and history was recorded by referring to the tree—there was the year, for instance, when one of the branches broke. And it served as winning post for the races they held. So it was that the tree remained a living symbol in the minds of young and old alike.

He, like so many others, had learned to respect the tree. It was the father of every family, the *shaykh* of the tribe, the fortress protecting the village. Every school trip had the tree as its destination. It was, quite simply, the place where everything ended.

The history teacher had once told them the following story:

"Our village," he'd said, "has an ancient history, and its people are renowned for their strength and courage. And they've always been proud of their great, strong tree, which has been the envy of all the other villages round about. Once two of these formed an alliance, deciding to attack our village and burn the tree while everyone was asleep. They hid behind the hills and waited for darkness to fall and people to sleep. Then they attacked the tree and set it on fire.

"When the muezzin woke to call to prayer, he knew at once this was no fire lit by wayfarers, but one started deliberately to burn up the tree, and he summoned the people, telling them their tree was in danger. They rushed out, carrying their weapons, and engaged with the attackers, who lost twenty men while ten died from our own village. We took five prisoners too, and these, as a punishment, had to water the tree every day for a year. After that incident, the people decided to name their village "The Tree." This is one of the many stories about the tree, and this is why you should take such pride in it."

And so he'd grown up with a sense of veneration for the tree, which had, over the years, become a symbol of pride and dignity. Even when he left the village and went to live in the city, he still felt the world was made up just of his village and its tree, and his love for both remained as strong as his love for his own family.

With each day that passed, he discovered new things, bigger by far than the world he'd left behind. He saw trees far larger than the tree in his village, minarets much taller than the single minaret of his village's sole mosque. The city seemed as great as the sea, with its lights, shopping centers, wide roads, and tall buildings.

The city came to fill his mind and heart; it conquered his senses. Yet still the village remained a firm and solid memory, unshaken by any doubt—even though the village itself, when he returned to visit it, looked so void and colorless compared with his vast new world. Then, little by little, the village began to slip from his memory and heart. He even sought to avoid recalling it, strove to keep himself busy and thrust any memories off, as people do when they want to forget particular people or places.

One day, as part of an educational trip organized by his science teacher, he visited the museum, and the teacher explained to them how they could tell the age of a tree by counting the circles inside its trunk. Amazed, he thought of the tree in his village, wondering how old it was. But surely, he thought, no one could tell unless the tree was cut down. He thought of cutting down the tree, imagined, even, that it actually had been cut down and he was counting the circles. The idea of this disturbed him, yet it crossed his mind more than once.

During one of his visits to the village, he stood gazing at the tree. It wasn't, he thought now, any different from other trees. In fact it was distinctly weak and dried up, looked quite commonplace. He couldn't bring himself, any longer, to feel veneration for it.

For a while he refused to recognize these feelings of disrespect for the tree, this sense of its insignificance; he preferred to keep it as a sacred myth cherished in his heart. The tree led him on to think of his village, so remote from any trace of development and civilization. Saddened by this, he resolved to help his village gain its share of development. He wrote a number of articles and sent them to newspapers. He spoke to the officials concerned. He even got the young people of his village together, urging them to press for its development. His efforts bore fruit, and the village won its share of attention.

After he'd graduated and embarked on a career, he didn't, nevertheless, forget about his village, which developed little by little, till, one day, it was decided a hospital should be built there. The best place for this, the surveyor decided, would be where the tree stood. The tree would have to be cut down.

The decision upset the people, who felt the hospital would only bring them bad luck; and, after a long debate, a committee was formed, made up of the educated people of the village. The surveyor stuck to his guns. The history teacher told him it would be a grave mistake, for the village itself was named after the tree, and the people took pride in the name. The mayor seconded the teacher's opinion. It would, he said, be very difficult to change the village's name. Then why not, the surveyor suggested, call it "The Ex-Tree Village"? But the Arabic teacher rejected the notion, saying this was grammatically incorrect. Another suggestion was to cut down the tree but keep the old name. The Quranic teacher, though, opposed this, saying it would foster blasphemy. Someone had the thought of rooting the tree up and re-planting it somewhere near the hospital, but the agriculture expert wouldn't hear of it; old trees, he explained, were difficult to transplant. Yet another idea was to keep the tree and build the hospital around it. This, the finance officer said, would add greatly to the expense; and besides, it would only be in the way of the doctors and patients, and bring insects into the hospital. Someone put forward the idea of a vote, but this was rejected out of hand, because voting was a heresy.

The health representative put his foot down. If, he said, they couldn't find a solution, he'd have no option but to build the hospital in the neighboring village, which meant they'd be at the mercy of these same neighbors, who (as the people knew well enough) greatly disliked them. He gave them a week to think the matter over and come to a decision. The week passed, but nothing had been decided. They were still arguing among themselves.

A year later, the people were passing by the tree on their way to the hospital. One thing had certainly got bigger—the graveyard to the west of the tree. In time the tree was standing right in the middle of the graveyard.

Abu Rashed

The typewriter tapped monotonously, and Abu Rashed sat in his chair listening pensively to the sound that had been familiar for more than thirty years now. Everything changed here except for the sound of the typewriter and the corners of the place. As he listened to the tapping from the next room, he wondered just how many letters and papers had been typed. There'd been quite a few typists working there; some had left, some had changed, some had just vanished, leaving behind them the tapping sound that filled his ears all day long, only stopping briefly now and then.

Thirty-five years had passed like a vision! For a while he dozed as if listening to them, his soul floating over the clouds of the past, and he felt a stab of pain as he remembered the lorry that had brought him from his village to the city, where he'd meant to spend just a week or so, but had ended up spending his whole life. All right, he wasn't satisfied, but that was fate! He'd found the city attractive, though, and had worked in various places before finally settling down here.

This wasn't his home, or where he lodged, or his office. It was something completely different. It was all his years rolled together, the storehouse of his memories, his whole history, so filled with events and talk; hundreds of faces, thousands of stories had passed by and gone, leaving him just the sounds of the typewriter, the teapot and the coffee-maker.

He'd had his happy days, days full of tenderness and respect and warm memories, with his bosses Abu Muhammad and Abu Said and Abu Khaled. Dozens of colleagues filled his memory; their images crowded it with varied colors, and their voices swept through his mind, arousing a blend of feelings that brought him close to tears.

The yellow bus that carried the employees, their talk, their jokes and remarks, the friendly atmosphere, the excursions—where had all that gone? There was nothing left now. Everything had gone; nothing remained in his memory but images like the shadows of sunset before darkness falls.

He sighed as he remembered Um Rashed.[1] How beautiful she'd been! The children had grown up now, the girls were married. Yes, everything had changed. Nothing was the same any more, except for himself and the sound of the typewriter. Suddenly he was overwhelmed with a mingled sorrow and satisfaction. He was a prisoner still, of this state that had crept up on him—or been stored inside him maybe, building up day by day till, suddenly, it had burst out.

He accepted the feeling wholly, sadness and all; he even felt a certain happiness, smiling to himself, consoling himself with the thought: "that's how life is." Surrendering to a deep stillness, like the stillness of drowsiness or sleep.

Suddenly the place was in turmoil. His Excellency had arrived! The whole office was shaking, even the sound of the typewriter was stilled. The bell rang. Coffee! Coffee! He leaped off his chair, poured a cup of coffee, then another cup. He got up and stood in position, his body leaning to one side like a pole about to fall. His Excellency the Director was writing, speaking on the phone, ringing the bell, talking to the secretary. And still Abu Rashed stood there, his legs growing stiff, his left hand frozen in its place as he grasped the handle of the coffee pot, his right hand ready to take the cup. For a long time he stood there. Then, at last, he said:

"Your coffee's getting cold, sir."

The Director turned, shot him a glance of disdain and disgust, then nodded. Abu Rashed leaned down, raised the cup of coffee and moved backward, feeling as though a hand, rough and merciless, was grasping at his wretched heart, filled, for so many years, with the pain such humiliations had brought. The worst of them all had come the day the Director told him to help him off with his *bisht* and hang it up each time he came into the office, then help him on with it again when he left.[2] He'd come close to refusing, but the hardships of life had helped him find the patience he needed.

Everything had changed since his old boss left; nothing was the same any more. This new director held an exalted degree from a foreign country. He'd lived a long time abroad and come home with a different way of thinking—a way that was neither western nor eastern. It was this nervous, unsettled blend, lacking any harmony or strength or balance, which made a person like that arrogant and inclined to look down on others. He couldn't create a friendly atmosphere at work, couldn't spur on his employees, who were floating in a totally different space while he sat trapped in his ivory tower.

His Excellency liked to drink his coffee slowly, while Abu Rashed waited on him, gazing at the office, the silent papers, the desk, the files, the colored telephones, the expensive pens and lamps, the artificial flowers and the heavy, silent sadness.

Abu Rashed tried to read the Director's name, engraved in ivory on a blue board with a gold frame—all quite meaningless alongside the quiet, stony heart of the man who sat there. This profound arrogance, Abu Rashed felt, blocked out the flow of light and happiness. Everything around this spot was paralyzed, sterile and pointless.

The ringing of the phone broke the heavy silence. His Excellency slowly picked up the receiver.

"Hello," he said. His tone was cold.

Then he gave a sudden start, and his voice changed. There were greetings! He made a signal to Abu Rashed to leave the room, and Abu

Abu Rashed

Rashed, once outside, closed the door behind him and sat back down on his chair. There he waited in total silence, a painful silence, of lingering old age and the weight of years.

Time was a heavy burden. The days hemmed in those who were old and fearful of a broken heart and body, approaching their seventies now. How wretched it is when the wings of the soul begin to break, the supports of the heart to cave in.

The bell rang. He jumped to go and take the cup from His Excellency, whose left arm was half stretched out, his head in a file, his right hand rustling the papers. The cup shook in his hand, then fell before Abu Rashed could stop it. His Excellency leaped up, startled and furiously angry. Abu Rashed picked up the cup.

"*Salamat*," he said. "*Salamat*."[3]

His Excellency, though, let fly with his tongue.

"You fool!" he stormed. "You're useless, the lot of you! This is an office, not an old people's home. Get out of here, or I'll—" Abu Rashed reached the door. "You're an idiot," His Excellency raved on. "Just stupid! You belong in the garbage can, not in a respectable office!"

Abu Rashed stood there, the words like knives stabbing him from his back into his heart. He turned, placed the coffee pot on a table in the middle of the room and walked quietly toward the door. Then all the pains of the years gathered in him: the forced patience, the buried anger exploded through all his heart and all his soul.

Suddenly this peaceful man became a lion.

His eyes turned red, every nerve in his body shook. He approached His Excellency, who looked on in disbelief, and tore off the man's glasses. The Director tried to push Abu Rashed off but fell back in his chair instead. Abu Rashed came close to slapping the man, then banging his head down on his glass-covered desk. But he didn't. He merely pushed him hard back, in a gesture brim full of hatred and contempt, then left him searching for his glasses.

Next Abu Rashed went straight to the typist and asked him to type as follows:

> Sir: I have served thirty-five years here, but cannot remain thirty seconds longer. I tender my resignation herewith.

With that he left the office, the typewriter still sounding behind him. He walked out of the Ministry door, and, turning to look behind him, saw the lofty palm tree towering over the gate. He was the one, he recalled, who'd planted it.

Then he walked down the long road, listening to his own footsteps, the footsteps of the years—the taps of the typewriter.

The Bird of Fury

As he stood at his bedroom window, overlooking the roof of the neighboring building, his eyes fell on a small bird standing on the antenna. The wind was blowing hard, shaking the antenna in every direction, and the bird tried to hide its head as some of its feathers were blown away.

At each new gust the bird took a firmer grip on the antenna, setting its body against the wind, but still the savage wind thrust and pulled, harder and harder, in every direction, while the bird stood firm.

The weather was cold and raindrops were thudding against the window, making it hard to see the small creature. Still, though, he felt the urge to keep watching this battle between the fierce wind and the tiny pile of feathers, over a body thin as a wheat stalk, which was facing such a mighty gale.

"Why this obstinacy?" he asked himself angrily. "Why doesn't the bird just fly off to the nearest hiding place and find some shelter? What's the secret of this bird's determination to face the wind, and the cold and rain?" Again and again he asked himself the question, staring at this stupid bird so stubbornly and patiently intent on facing the gale.

At each new gust, too, the bird let out angry sounds, as if defending its place with body and voice alike, as if shrieking in the face of the wind: "No! No!"

The wind calmed down somewhat, and still the bird didn't move. For a moment he thought it would fly off, the cold wind defeated; but it didn't. It stood motionless on the antenna, as if waiting for the wind to start blowing all over again.

He pulled down the curtain and went back to watching TV, where they were showing scenes of a great flooded river and the water destroying the houses and fields. He saw some people holding on to large trees, others standing on the roofs of houses and tall buildings, while still others gathered near the sandbags used as barricades to hold the all-destroying river at bay.

The commentator went on sadly reading the report of the heavy losses caused by the hurricane, announcing the number of souls and properties lost on account of the raging flood. Helicopters filled the sky, searching for the injured and displaced, and those cut off by the flood. Filled with pity for these people, he pressed the pad on the remote control to change the channel, and saw a squadron of jet fighters with clouds of smoke streaming from their engines as they shook and burned the land beneath them with their bombs. There was a great mass of people and animals and cars fleeing, all being driven out by this flood of fury toward the river of the unknown. There were fires and smoke and cries for help filling the place, and yet even they were drowned out by the bombing and the fiery flames.

He tried to scream, but he couldn't.
He tried to weep, but he couldn't.
He tried to speak out, but he couldn't!

Wishing only to flee, he pressed the remote control once more, to find a number of people negotiating an agreement. One side had faces like wolves and eyes as cunning as foxes'. The other had flabby faces and noses like small rubber hoses, together with dim swollen eyes like the eyes of sick seagulls. The two sides exchanged hollow smiles, then solemnly shook one another's hands. An agreement was about to be signed, and he recalled the Palestinian proverb: "Such an agreement needs such a signature."

"And now," the commentator said, "the agreement's about to be signed. This is a historic hour indeed." An hour, a signature, a place. A line of poetry sprang into his mind:

> Life may be worth but a single hour;
> Land may be worth but a single place.

He raised his head and let out the rotten air that had seeped into his very consciousness, choking him almost. He ran to the window, his mind spurring his body on. He opened the curtain to find the bird still there. It was motionless, still in the same spot.

Wind and lightning, thunder and rain! This

bird refused to abandon its challenging dance. He couldn't believe his eyes. Could this small body hold such incredible force, to fight the strong forces of nature? Did the bird have some instinctive love of struggle? Or did its soul conceal some mighty strength that overcame the difficulties and hard times no matter what?

God! How could this small, frail body turn itself to a spearhead, ready to cut open the breast of the wild wind should it ever seek to blow the small body away? A heroic bird indeed.

He laughed at the sight of this bird's strength, then thought mockingly of those weakling negotiators, with their flabby faces and their dim eyes like the eyes of sick seagulls. Then, he turned to the defiant bird and saluted him.

The Composition Lesson

"The Soviet Union's collapsed," Hamad told his friend, "and no one's shed any tears. So don't think anyone's going to cry just because your son failed his exam."

He caught his breath before he spoke. It was such a hot day he thought the tank in his car would explode with the soaring temperature. As for the rage built up inside Saleh, that too was looking for an outlet to burst out from.

"The wretched boy failed," he said, wiping the sweat from his face. "In composition! Can you believe he couldn't pass that, the fool? What more can I do?" he went on. "Just tell me! I've spent a fortune on private teachers for him, and what's the result? Well, you've heard it. The funny thing is, he passed all the other exams with top marks—then he failed a ridiculously easy subject like this. The shock knocked me right back. I nearly broke his head for him. Please, try and find a tutor to teach him composition."

Hamad passed him a glass of cold water.

"Calm down," he said. "There's no point killing yourself over it. Your son isn't the first to fail a test, and he certainly won't be the last. Didn't I tell you the Soviet Union—"

Saleh became irritated.

"What do I have to do with the cursed Soviet Union?" he broke in. "I tell you about my son, and you talk to me about the Soviet Union!"

"My friend," Hamad replied, "I really don't know what's the matter with you. I'm just trying to make things easier for you, by comparing this "disaster" to the one that's hit nearly half the population of the world—a military and ideological collapse together. Communism's collapsed, along with millions of people who believed in it, read its declarations and books, knew them by heart even. Books like *Das Kapital*. Down went Karl Marx, and with him went more than a billion communists who believed in his ideology and his philosophy. And you're raising hell just because your son failed his exam!"

As Saleh entered the room, Abdul Karim was sitting in the corner by the bookshelves, and he greeted Saleh with a mere wave of the hand. He was absorbed in his reading. Abdul Karim was famous among his friends. Some called him "the philosopher," others reckoned he was obsessed. He was known for his love of reading and the way he'd ridicule his friends' views and thoughts.

Hamad was still talking about communism. When he'd finished, Abdul Karim cleared his throat, taking off the thick spectacles from his small eyes and hawk-like nose. He banged the table in front of him.

"Look, Hamad," he said. "Communism hasn't collapsed and it never will. The Soviet Union may have failed, but communism will live on."

"You're not short of confidence, I must say," Hamad answered. "All this has happened, and you still don't believe communism's collapsed, that it's gone for ever! I don't understand you. Is it this philosophy, rooted right down inside your head, that makes you too proud to accept defeat? To admit you've failed?"

"You know better than anyone," Abdul Karim retorted, "just why the Soviet Union broke up."

"Ah, here we go. It's all the fault of the CIA and western intelligence!"

"Well, you can't deny the sheer impact of the West's fight against Russia. What with the cold war and all the military and economic blocs."

"Great! So, the West won and the Soviet Union lost. The phantom of communism, to everyone's surprise, faded away just like that. If communism had really been that strong, the West could never have pierced it and destroyed it."

Abdul Karim was irritated now.

"Men like you," he said, "with your degrees from the West, are just sick, obsessed with your love of all things western. You've been taken in, by a fake image! You're in love with freedom and leisure facilities, with shopping malls and all the consumer goods you can buy. The trouble is, you don't have any philosophy or human goals. The western mentality's built on glamour, on shares, on promotion. Westerners may look respectable on the outside, but the truth is they're dupes, slaves long since sold to the banks. They're bound hand and foot by taxes and loans, from the day they're born to the day they die. By the struggle to pay for luxuries you're pleased to call development and progress. Their souls are dead to all humanity and pity. Their brains have turned to calculators, their hearts to a wallet filled with plastic cards that help them spend their money."

"And the Soviet citizens, they were living in paradise, were they?"

Throughout all this Saleh was watching his two friends with confusion and suppressed emotion. He wanted to say something, but Hamad didn't give him the chance.

"Listen, Abdul Karim," Hamad said. "Communism failed because of a flaw at its very heart. It was a closed system, where you couldn't even breathe properly. Russia was just one big prison surrounded by iron walls, where the "comrades" persecuted the people for seventy years. Yes! For seventy years the comrades ate the sweets while the people ate the dry bread and wore old shoes. The comrades were driven in expensive western limousines, while the people rode on donkeys, or drove cars that looked like donkeys. The "Party" lived in palaces and the people lived in houses more like boxes."

"Hamad!" Saleh shouted. "Abdul Karim! Stop it, for pity's sake!"

But Hamad was still intent on putting an end to all the stupidity.

"You ought to wake up, Abdul Karim," he said. "You're still a prisoner of ideology. You're hypnotized by a dead theory, duped by all those

The Composition Lesson

blasphemous books. Open up to the world, won't you? How much longer are you going to see it through that distorted lens of yours? I honestly feel sorry for you, and all the others like you, who think communism's just going through some 'normal phase in its evolution.'

"Take a look at Russia, and Germany, and a lot of the Eastern European countries. Look at the world around you. Castro, the Chief Rabbi of Communism, visited the Vatican and kissed the Pope's hand, asked for his blessing and forgiveness. Don't let your pride blind you. The ones I pity are the millions who were tortured and executed because of this devilish ideology."

Saleh was getting heartily sick of his friends and their wretched argument. Abdul Karim, though, still went on, his voice shaking with anger.

"All that happened because of the western intelligence services! You talk about the victims of communism, but you don't say a word about the brutality of the West, which uses the most squalid methods to eat up people's resources and drag them into crises and wars and embargoes — deprives them of bread and medicines even. If only communism could be given the chance, just once, to express itself!"

"Hamad!" Saleh shouted. "What about the composition lesson? I came to you looking for an answer, and you end up arguing with this idiot here."

"Yes," Abdul Karim went on, ignoring Saleh's remark. "If communism had only had the chance to express itself democratically, without being hemmed in by the West and its conspiracies, then the Soviet Union would never have collapsed. Look, won't you, at China and its struggle against poverty and sickness and ignorance, in the face of all the restrictions imposed by the West? Look at the way it's fought to build a balanced society, without natural resources, and with a vast population too, bigger than the whole of the West's put together. There's an example of how pure and right this ideology is, when it's only given the chance to function properly."

Hamad was beginning to lose all hope of convincing his friend.

"Russia," he insisted, "collapsed, all of a sudden, from a heart attack. As for China, it's sick and on the way out too."

"The composition lesson!" Saleh yelled. He went almost crazy as Abdul Karim waved a dismissive hand. "Hamad, please, I beg you. This man's just an idiot. He's like someone praising the courage of some dead knight, as he waits for him to come back from battle. He's stupid, that's all, an idiot who won't let his illusions go."

"And since when did mules have brains?" Abdul Karim retorted. "Why don't you leave talking about thoughts and ideology and just go to hell? You're an empty drum, good for nothing except filling your stomach, while your head's left with nothing inside. If your son failed his composition test, it's because you're an imbecile. Why don't you just keep quiet?"

Saleh leaped up and ripped off his *igal*, ready to hit Abdul Karim, but Hamad grabbed hold of him.[4]

"Let me break his head for him," Saleh yelled, still struggling to get free. "The dim-witted hedgehog!"

Sensing things were getting serious, Hamad thrust Saleh out into the hall.

"Look," he said, "you know what Abdul Karim's like. He's a decent fellow, but you shouldn't argue with him and work him up."

Hamad was doing his best to hold himself in and wipe the sweat from his forehead with his *ghutra*.[5]

"Abdul Karim," Saleh said, "isn't a 'decent fellow.' He's a devious type, and I keep away from him as much as I can. This is all your fault. I came to you hoping you might make things easier for me, and you just end up making them worse. You launched into this argument, on communism and the West, and forgot all about God! I wanted you to help me find a composition tutor, and we end up getting involved with this fool here. If my son fails, Hamad, then I've failed too. It will be living proof I'm incapable of making a success of him. Heaven help us poor parents! We burn so as to light up the road for our children, and all they do is stumble."

There was a silence. Hamad felt now he'd been wrong to start that argument with Abdul Karim and get Saleh involved too. He hadn't, he reflected, shown his friend much sympathy or been much help in finding a solution to his son's problem. As for Saleh, he was plunged deep in thought, feeling regret and remorse together. From the window overlooking the garden Hamad could see the sun setting, and sense the smell of greenery and water filling the place, as if the warm breeze was giving way to a cool one that mingled with the sweet fragrance of the trees.

"Why don't we go out in the garden?" he said.

They sat under the apple tree, where a few butterflies were flitting around. Trying to reduce the tension with a joke, he said:

"Do you think your son will turn out like Newton?"

Saleh cursed Newton, and Newton's parents as well.

"But he was a great man," Hamad said. "He discovered the law of gravity."

"Gravity was there before Newton and his rotten apple," Saleh retorted.

"That rotten apple was a pretty momentous one," Hamad said seriously. "It helped Newton discover gravity. Don't think falling always means failure. If that apple hadn't fallen down, Newton would never have brought off his discovery. And if your son's failed his composition test, he still might manage to—"

Their conversation was interrupted by Abdul Karim, who walked into the garden to join them. He was polishing his glasses with his *ghutra*, and, not seeing the steps going down, he slipped and fell.

Saleh leaped in the air and laughed.

"Marx's apple!" he said. "Marx's apple's fallen down!"

The Mirage

The sun was burning down with its rays, turning the sky to a silver dome. The deadly drought embraced the place. Dried trees were dotted here and there, covered with dust and shabby as the face of death, their damp roots struggling for survival. Amazing how these trees fought against uprooting and thirst, the burning sun and the poisonous wind!

The small African rue tree was the only sign of life here. You might say it was made to grow in the midst of hell itself. Nafi couldn't, for all his skill, cross the sandy expanse. He'd known well enough the difficulty and danger of crossing where even skilled drivers ventured only at night, when the sand had grown harder; and now his love of adventure, or recklessness rather, had left him with his Datsun stuck in the sand. He strove to get it out by taking the sand from in front of the two sets of wheels, but that only made the car sink deeper still, till the doors themselves were part submerged.

Looking around him, he could see only drought and despair. In the distance was the mirage pouring like water crossed by wild horses. The mirage was everywhere, as if he'd reached an island in the sea of hell.

He could feel the sun's burning rays piercing into his skull. He pictured a small palm tree full of dates, with a running stream nearby and plenty of shade. The hot air was filling his lungs now, and his mouth was as dry as his car's exhaust pipe.

It was the smell of gasoline that finally brought him to himself. Once more he looked all around, but to no avail. The only thing he could see was a camel's body partially buried in the sand. Then, far away, he spotted a moving shadow. God! Could it be a car? He didn't dare believe his eyes, for everything seemed like a mirage now—like false phantoms, flitting in all directions, now appearing, now vanishing.

He watched carefully, seeing how the phantom came ever nearer. Could it be death? What else could there be in this deadly desert?

The black camel halted, watching from a distance, while Nafi, back in his car now, watched too, waiting hopefully for it to approach. Cautiously the camel drew nearer. Camels are used enough to cars. They've seen people bring water, food, and hay in cars. On the other hand, people have taken camels in cars to be slaughtered in the city.

This camel was fearful and suspicious. Nafi, for his part, was boiling, soaking wet in the heat, yet with his tongue as dry as a wooden board. As he opened the door, the camel continued to inspect the car; and it went on looking as Nafi's feet sank into the sand. Nafi took a first step toward it, and the camel took a step backward. Nafi moved back to the car. Here, he knew, was his only hope of escaping this ocean of thirst and heat. The camel watched cautiously.

Nafi took two steps forward, and this was enough to scare the camel and make it run off as fast as it could, leaving a cloud of dust and sand behind it. Then it stopped, looked at Nafi and started walking back, but didn't once venture to approach the car again.

As his strength failed, Nafi began to lose hope. He'd come to terms with his destiny, with thirst and sweat. He was a man dying for a fistful of pennies worth not one good draught of fresh air. It was a hundred note that had led him to this crazy act, to cross this sea of sand with its boiling waves.

The sun was growing weaker now, and the wind blew from all directions, as Nafi still looked around him, seeking some way out of the hell. But there was no sign of life in the desert, except for that crazy camel.

"Could it be the beast they talk about in the stories?" Nafi thought to himself. "Or a phantom maybe? Nothing lives in this desert. There's no water. Only the mirage and the phantoms. Just this camel—or phantom—or beast."

As the heat lessened still further, Nafi climbed the dunes to see what lay around him, hoping to see a phantom, or some sign of life. But all he saw was the desert, vast enough to swallow the whole universe. Despair filled his heart, and raging fire. This desert, he thought, might soon become his grave. He was going to end up just like that dead camel he'd seen before. Then, next morning, he'd be eaten by the eagles and falcons. It was a nightmare—and a fearful reality! Here, in this desert, the real and the imaginary coalesced to form one bitter truth.

The sun was setting like a ball of fire. He'd never seen it look that way before. Perhaps it was because he'd never watch another sunset. Darkness crept into the empty waste, and the sky was lit with sparkling diamonds. For all his despair and sense of death's nearness, the cool breeze made him feel better, and the sight of the lovely sky restored his faith. Above him, he felt, was a whole universe full of life, with its shooting stars, its burning comets and circling planets. It was as though he was seeing the sky for the first time.

"How blind we all are," he said to himself. "I've never in my whole life seen anything so splendid. Maybe it's because I'm going to die tonight. Or maybe it's heaven's way of welcoming my soul."

Nafi felt strong once more, felt the urge to overcome despair and sorrow. Perhaps the shining stars had kindled the light of hope in his heart. He decided to leave the car and walk. But where? He considered going back, but he'd already crossed tens of kilometers, and the sun would rise and set again before he ever reached his village. Going on, though, would be still more difficult and exhausting. He could walk left or right, but had no idea where he might end up. Which way should he go? He couldn't decide.

Finally, he decided to go where his feet led him. He took the small bag—the cause of his ill-fated trip—adjusted his *ghutra*, then, as he was about to start out, suddenly remembered his car key. Should he take it or not? He thought long about it, then decided to take the key. As he reached out to grasp it, his hand accidentally hit the light key on the dashboard, and the lights came on. To his surprise, there was the black camel, the beast, the phantom, staring straight into the lights, startled and fearful.

Wonderful! Nafi walked slowly, noiselessly through the darkness, like a wolf, while the camel continued to look into the lights. Then, like a leopard, he leaped onto the camel and held on tight to its neck. The camel ran off like a shooting rocket, into the heart of darkness. Nafi felt as though his head was about to touch the stars. Was he on a spaceship or a ship of the desert?

That morning the village that had woken, for the past forty years, to the sound of car horns, woke to the sound of a running camel. Who would ever have believed such a thing?

Redemption

The last thing he'd expected to hear, when he first turned on the recorder, was this patriotic song. He hadn't been using the machine, which had lain for years now amidst old books, beneath the thick dust of time.

The song whipped up a storm of feelings, buried long and deep in a heart that had grown stagnant. A person could hold conflicting emotions and pains, which would pile up inside him and stay motionless there, like a hibernating snake, or like a landmine ready to blow up at the slightest move or touch. He felt as though a tornado had struck him, sweeping away all that inner stillness.

As a child the song had moved him, had brought out a sense of pride and honor, a rejection of shame and servility. It had wakened a thirst for revenge, evoked feelings of chivalry and courage. Even his father, who had no time for singing at all, had never minded listening, again and again, to that particular song—even he had been moved by its call for redemption.

He stood, transfixed, among all these old belongings, while the recorder went on playing the song as though it were a corpse brought suddenly back to life. Things could change, he realized that now, could disappear almost. He saw how total action could turn to total stillness.

The books—the recorder—the place that had once been bustling and alive—all these things had been given over to silence. Who would have believed history could be so silenced and altered? Who would have believed all the ideals, all the rights and principles, no longer had power to speak? All those books invoking human rights, all those volumes of poetry, all those newspapers? The books and poets were quiet now, as if drugged. And he'd been very quiet too. It was the recorder that had brought him face to face with this silent assembly.

Leafing through the books and novels so long abandoned, he felt a sense of shame. He opened a volume of poetry and read a poem. There, staring up at him, were his notes and remarks on a poem he'd once known by heart. He tried to recite some of the lines now, but his memory failed him.

His conscience pricked unbearably as he read through. He'd betrayed his cause. How could he have forgotten all those lines? How could the phoenix have turned to ashes? How could he have neglected those hallowed books, which had taught him everything about his just and holy cause?

He felt like someone accused and guilty, in a courtroom surrounded by the friendly faces of those he'd harmed, against whom he'd practiced the vilest human abuse.

But was it really his fault? Suppose he'd memorized all the lines in those books? Could he have helped win a victory or prevent a defeat? He was confused now. What was happening to him? Was he just trying to justify himself? He belonged to this nation. How could he have surrendered so easily, in such an abject way, a right, historical, religious and cultural, that he'd been brought up to cherish?

He should have stood up for his beliefs, for his cause. Just like those books that had preserved their sentiments and ideals over so many years. Just as the song had preserved its soul and its sad melody.

Listening to the song once more, he realized how his hope was broken, his soul chained fast so as to leave him half blind, barely able to see enough to keep him from tumbling in this abyss. And yet what could be harder than that other sudden fall, which had brought everything crashing down with it?

Some of the intellectuals had started defending the enemy, bluntly and crudely, showing how their loyalty was to personal interest and not to homeland. He tried to run away and forget, but he couldn't. The images were streaming now: images of defeat and disgrace, boldness and courage, the proud and the broken. Images of battlefields and martyrs. A history filled with heroic tales, defeats and crises. Images of true, honorable people and of traitors. Images of a homeland broadening out beyond the sunrise, and of a homeland rent and destroyed.

His soul was torn apart now, as if by some wild bird. He woke to the voice of his daughter singing along with the song.

Poor girl! And poor him! The sight of his daughter left him more frightened still. Did this young girl know just what the words meant and why they were sung? Did she know this song was one weapon among many, wielded to prevent the slaughter of children, of the land and his dignity, of all who were murdered? A weapon, land and dignity.

Would this girl enjoy a better future, one ensuring such a nightmare never came again? Or was her future doomed? That future looked bleak. Still the song went on, and the girl danced, and his soul worked to destroy itself.

He turned off the recorder. His heart was wounded and bleeding now. He switched on the radio, to hear an announcement in Arabic:

"A Palestinian terrorist has blown up a military bus. Five Israeli soldiers were martyred."

A Palestinian terrorist! Five Israeli soldiers martyred!

He switched off the radio and turned on the recorder. The singer was singing of "redemption," his daughter was dancing, and he sank, paralyzed, into a pit of disgrace and sorrow.

Shabash!

"*Shabash! Shabash!*" Those were the words the old man kept repeating. He was wearing a blue jacket on top of his white robe, and a white turban covered his hair.

The small Chevrolet, swept away by the flood that had hit the town the night before, was stuck in the mud. The driver, Uthman— who'd emerged unharmed by a miracle—had ridiculed the people's warnings.

"I'll cross that river," he'd told them. "I don't care if it's the Nile!"

And so he'd driven through the flood, only to end up stuck. All his attempts to get the car out had failed, as its wheels sank deep into the sludge.

Uthman, though, hadn't given up. He'd opened the car's hood and started drying the electric wires in the hope the car would start. Suddenly he'd heard calls from people near and far: "The valley! The valley!"

But Uthman, or Usman as he was sometimes called, had paid no attention, unaware the flood had crashed against the two sides of the valley, right up to the moment it started sweeping him away, leaving him no chance to escape. He'd tried to swim, crying for help, but the flood had drowned out his desperate shouts.

He'd been pushed, pulled and tossed about. Then, at last, he'd seen the branch of a tree, a gift from God! Clinging to the branch, he'd contrived to reach the land. It was a miracle. No one could believe Uthman had somehow come out safe from the flood. The car, though, had been swept away. It was buried in a sludgy hill now, only the dented roof visible.

Next day, when the afternoon prayer was over, the people of the village gathered to pull out the car. They took away the piles of sand that had buried it and tied a rope to the fender. Then, as the men, young and old, tugged on the rope, the old man kept repeating: "*Shabash*!"

The owner of the car was a very rich man, who'd bought a ranch and built an enormous mansion that had all the luxuries, including a cinema. The villagers didn't even know what a cinema was. They only heard the sounds of men, women, shooting, crying, singing, that came from the place late at night.

Ibrahim, the young intellectual of the village, told them it was called a "cinemo"—he'd seen one before, he said, at ARAMCO in Dhahran. He took delight in slipping in at nightfall, with the connivance of the guard, and watching the films screened on the white wall in the big courtyard. But it all seemed like magic even to him, and he found it difficult to explain to the villagers what the cinema was all about.

Still the car was buried in the sludge, and still

the men, young and old, struggled to pull it out. Some pushed, while others tried to free a way for the wheels. But the car was stuck deep in the wet sand, and its inside was filled with stones and water. Finally, after endless pushing and pulling, the car emerged, broken and damaged. As the people finally pulled it out, the old man saluted them. "*Shabash*!" he said.

"What does '*shabash*' mean?" one young boy asked himself. What *was* the meaning of this strange word? It had a nice ring to it, and the old man used it whenever he wanted to encourage people. The lad would have liked to get him to explain it, but he wasn't bold enough to ask.

The old man had a very solemn air, with his dark skin and his white beard and mustache. His lined forehead was hard and strong—you could almost have used it to sharpen a knife. He wasn't especially tall, but he was strongly built, a very distinctive kind of person combining qualities of the Bedouin and the townsman. Some said he looked after the horses at the rich man's ranch, others that he'd once fought in the Turkish Army. No one really knew him. He came together with the cinema, the grand cars, Usman the driver, "*Shabash*" and the empty colored bottles scattered in front of the ranch gate.

All these things stopped the lad asking the old man what the word meant. Even so, he could use it and spread it among his classmates, and his brothers, and the boys of the quarter. Whenever he wanted to encourage somebody, he'd say: "*Shabash*!" The word soon spread and, as people started using it, the boy felt as if he'd invented it and promoted it himself. He even heard a teacher using it to encourage one of his students!

He was proud of himself, that he'd been able to spread the use of a new word, though he was afraid someone, some day, might ask him what the word actually meant. But, strangely enough, no one ever did. For fear of showing ignorance, no doubt. Or was it the fascination with everything that's new, or some other reason he'd never know?

By the time he was grown up, the old man no longer lived in the village. The word, though, was still being used. The boy himself stopped saying it, but it lived on in his memory along with the distant images of his village and its people.

"*Shabash* to the village."

"*Shabash* to the old man."

"Shabash!"

The Tunnel

He flung down the shovel and looked at his bleeding hands.

"Get up," he told his son, "and start digging. My hands are swollen. There's only a bit left to dig.

"I've been digging since I was little more than a lad, and I've faced every kind of difficulty and hardship. I've faced heavy rocks, but still I've kept on digging. The shovels would break, but my resolution never broke. My arms grew tired from overwork, as fire sparked from digging those hard rocks. My strength would fail; but never my will and my resolve.

"I never thought of putting down the shovel. There's not just friendship between the two of us—there's union and total harmony. The shovel goes on as my life goes on, as my ancestors' lives went on before me.

"I'll fall and die maybe, but the shovel will go on digging and striking. It's the testament passed on from fathers to sons. When my father fell dead, I took the shovel from his hand. I didn't panic, or rush to dig his grave. I just moved his body to one side and kept on digging. Our fathers have been digging in this tunnel for hundreds of years. They'd go on digging however harsh conditions grew; not once did they abandon their shovels or their work. They passed through wars and hard times, through disasters and pain, and none of it, for a single moment, stopped them from digging on. In fact they'd help one another. Whenever an arm grew tired, there was always a strong, fresh arm ready to grab the shovel and go on digging. This tunnel's the road to a better life, to a dream. With each step forward, we come nearer to fulfilling the miracle, fulfilling the promise and God's satisfaction.

"Our ancestors lived in different places, yet they'd dig as one. Some used shovels, some dug with their bare hands—yes, their bare hands! Hands can dig their way through rocks too, as long as the will and the resolution are there. Some dug with their money, some with their long prayers and some with their cleverness and wit— that was the most effective shovel of all in digging this sacred tunnel, for a full two thousand years.

"The tunnel's witnessed the defeat of strongholds and countries and kingdoms. The stories of the cleverness used in digging are known only to those deeply versed in the tunnel's secret history.

"Dig, son, with God's help and the blessings of our ancestors. Dig! Dig, and invoke mercy on all those who've worked in this tunnel over so many centuries. You've reached the end of the road now. Hope's at hand and the long journey almost over.

"Don't ever give up or despair; for despair

can penetrate wills. It can weaken resolve and destroy nations.

"Son, when you make a breach, from this long tunnel, you'll be fortunate and blessed indeed. When you reach the door at the other end, with your own hands, then you'll have fulfilled God's promise and your ancestors' dream.

"You're lucky, son, that the earth you're digging is so moist and easy to work. Dig with hands and shovel alike, just as your ancestors did, to win God's satisfaction. The road's one, the goal's one, and the means should be one too, above all when you're digging deep inside. Let's leave technology for digging the outer channels. Remember, we were the ones who invented technology and mastered it. With technology we helped make everything move and fly, and we dug our outer channels; and so we entered the banks, yes, the banks, the parliaments, the organizations, the radio and TV stations. Don't we own most of the TV channels abroad? We could only achieve all this with the blessings of this inner, sacred tunnel visible to no one, of which no one except for you, the chosen people, and myself, is aware.

"There are tunnels, my dear son, that can't be dug with modern machines, no matter how advanced—especially those tunnels that dig through the pride and honor of your enemies."

The father's words spurred the young man on to dig with a will. He would, he felt, be fortunate indeed when he once made that first breach at the end of the tunnel. Whenever he recalled his father's words and pronouncements, his resolution to win this great honor would grow stronger. Still he dug, without once growing lazy or tired, and the sound of his digging echoed ever stronger.

In time, people began talking of the sounds they heard from the depths of the earth. At first they heard the sounds just at night, but then they'd hear him digging at different times, especially while they were praying at the holy mosque; the imam would linger over the prayer, so as to try and work out where the sound was coming from. Finally the sound grew so strong the mosque's very pillars and minaret and dome would quake.

Confusion reigned in the Holy City, as everyone talked of these strange happenings. People in those parts are easily astonished by anything new, and, as usual, they all disagreed over what was going on in their city. They concluded, finally, that it was caused by something called the "tunnel."

Some said this tunnel was an affront to their dignity, others that it was a relentless invasion of the whole nation. Some saw it as a living symbol of the hollowness of our existence; others as a giant trap into which all their mosques and homes would tumble, making it a graveyard for future generations.

Finally confusion gave way to loud voices, and these in turn gave way to radio stations and TV channels, to newspapers and magazines. The intellectuals gathered at a place called "Copenhagen," where those attending all had different faces and forms, and were from different races. The Chairman was an old man, his face turned black with age. He wore black sunglasses, and he had a face like an elderly ape's. Next to him sat a short, ugly man with untidy hair—his face was like the ape's backside.

After they'd made their speeches and drunk their toasts, they decided to delete the word "tunnel" from every dictionary, just as they'd deleted the word "conspiracy" before. They even decided to use the "veto" against any action that might run contrary to their decisions. Crucially, though, people had decided to stop work, to close the schools and shops, and to gather in the city square till the whole situation became clear. An old, fat man with a round face stood up before the crowd, amid total silence. All eyes and cameras and microphones were focused on him. At that very moment, the young man in the tunnel made a great breach at its end, seeing daylight after so long. The first thing to catch his eye was the Wailing Wall. Then, looking beyond, he saw the open sky and a most fertile land, a land rich with its rivers and oil and honey. He saw a mountain where houses were being demolished by machines, and he saw people screaming and fleeing and dying. He heard voices crying: "Victory! Success!"

He lifted his head to heaven.

"Hey, father!" he cried. "I've opened the tunnel. I've fulfilled heaven's promise and won God's satisfaction!"

The Tunnel

The young man gazed at the crowds gathered there. Then he heard the old, fat man say:

"'We have filled the land with our men; we shall fill the sea with our ships. 'It's a wonder, by God, that I find you all gathered here today, seeking to know the secret of the tunnel. It needs an expert to tell you the truth about it.

"The tunnel, ladies and gentlemen, brings to mind the lizard the Bedouins once hunted and ate in the desert, which looks like a rat but with a longer tail. This lizard grinds its food. It's a most intelligent creature. It usually digs its home in the ground, making one main entrance and a number of secret tunnels it can use to flee any danger. It's a cunning creature indeed, like all those cunning people we call hypocrites. People nowadays see hypocrisy as a kind of art.

"People used to say: 'When an animal dies, it's finished. And a cause dies when the people defending it die.' Yes, my dear ladies and gentlemen, this is the simple truth about the tunnel. Now, that's all cleared up, I imagine, so please go back to your work and homes, and may God be with you all."

That night the people returned home satisfied, and they slept soundly. There are, though, well-informed people who say work's under way on further tunnels, with new dimensions and a new direction.

The Novel

"I must have been reading for quite a while," he thought, taking a sip of the tea that was cold now. He thought of warming up the tea, but couldn't find the energy. The truth was, he was reading a new novel and was totally gripped by the events described in it. He felt as if he was living alongside the characters, day by day, and he'd come to realize the greatness of this author who could make his readers react to them like that, feeling their joy and anger and sadness.

Readers know none of a novel's events are true. But still they enjoy tricking themselves, convincing themselves they live in a reality contrived by the author as he sits writing at his desk. How can we be deceived so badly? Are we going back, maybe, to our innocent childhood feelings, with all their weakness and strength, to emotions that react without reservation? If so, then the child inside us is still awake, and some mighty superpower has grown there too, striving to overshadow the living child within.

The author, he was positive, was just toying with his readers, who in turn gave him large quantities of their feelings and time.

"What a fool I must be," he thought. "And what fools all readers are. Are we crazy? Look at me, for instance. I never tell a lie, and I hate every sort of deceit. And yet I find myself giving up reason and feeling alike to a professional liar; to a charlatan who fashions falsehoods and creates myths. If my best friend had tried to trick me like that, I would have broken with him long ago. And yet I've fallen in love with all these story makers!"

Still holding the novel, he lay down and tried to figure out what made people so weak, what allowed them to be gripped, just like that, by mere stories and myths and fairy tales.

Did these contrived stories somehow serve to fulfill human desires? Or did they help compensate for all the things we couldn't achieve in real life? Real strength, surely, lay in telling the truth, in voicing your opinion and fighting for your beliefs. Strength mattered in all its forms, whether in some steel structure or in a lion roaring in the jungle. The strength of the mind couldn't be reflected in myths and blasphemy.

Gazing up at the ceiling, he felt as though he'd drifted into a number of different worlds, each thronged with activities of its own, which his mind couldn't grasp. It was like seeing a dream or a movie full of action and romance, which made you feel, in the same moment, relaxed and beautiful and ugly.

Still he reflected, searching his soul for secrets buried deep inside, facing the most confusing, irritating questions; they hammered constantly at his head before settling, at last, in the depths of his mind and soul and consciousness.

How could people be, at once, so strong and so weak? How did we speak, weep, become hurt? Was strength really something so great? Was there really something called "being weak," or had we invented the feeling? Did we help make evil strong and virtue weak—so that tears, forgiveness, purity were seen as marks of weakness, killing, tyranny and cruelty as signs of strength?

He shuddered as he thought of all the atrocious murders people committed, while weeping at the death of a pet. People could, at one and the same time, steal and spend money like water, get furious and be quiet, betray and be loyal, believe and disbelieve, love and hate. He felt lost and depressed.

He was still holding the novel. "I've let it get to me," he thought. "I don't even know who the author is. I've no idea where he is at this moment. He might be watching a football match, or talking to a friend, or maybe reading the newspaper. Maybe he's suffering with a headache—but I bet he's not suffering as much as I am!

"Who am I? What is a novel? Who is the author? What's my connection with this stranger? I know him as an author, but nothing of him as a person. He's the creator of all these events and characters, these words and feelings, truths and lies. And, above all, he's made me a part of his written world. I live with his characters. I feel happy, I get upset, I even go into battle. I long for victory, and sometimes for defeat. I love some of the characters and hate others.

"The author's quite simply made me part of his novel, as though he wanted to test me in some way. Why do I feel so confused? Suppose I flung the book away, before I'd finished reading it. Would that be a strong thing to do? If I tore up every single page, would I be getting my own back on the author? And what if I go on reading? Will that amount to total despair?

"Whether or not I liked the novel, whether or not I believed everything the author wrote, if I burned the book even—none of that would change the fact that the novel does exist, and so does the author.

"Shall I switch off the light and go to sleep? Or shall I get up and make some tea? I must have been feeling listless and sleepy to have thoughts like these."

At midnight he gave a sigh of pain, as he read of his hero's defeat in the last line of the novel.

The Family Home

Usually the village, surrounded by its palm trees in the desert, slept early. That night, though, it lay awake.

Saad bin Saleh was about to leave, but not for the capital or some other city—he was leaving the whole country! Nor was he leaving for an Arab country, but for a western one; and not for a holiday, or for a few days or even months, but for several years.

Saad's home was filled with visitors. Some came to wish him well, others to say goodbye, while others grieved to see him leave. His mother, though, was more frightened, more apprehensive than the rest, weeping till there were no tears left to shed, while his father, for all his attempts to appear strong and composed, couldn't hide the pain behind his weak smile. Saad was going at dawn. He was leaving the country to finish his higher education in a western country. It was a night of tears, filled with overwhelming emotion.

When the plane landed, Saad followed the other passengers, afraid of getting lost in the big, complicated airport. He was relieved when he finally left it. He'd managed one of the main hurdles, as people saw it, facing every newcomer.

On the way he was stunned by the beautiful scenery—the greenness, the trees and woods, hills and rivers. He was surprised, too, to see so many villages and towns, and people bustling around. It was as though the whole country was one great city, its various parts separated by vast gardens.

The language institute wasn't as he'd expected or imagined. He'd thought an institute like that, in a western country, would be better organized and equipped. Instead he discovered, to his surprise, that his high school premises back home were more attractively built and furnished.

He lay down on the small bed, in the small room in the family home where he was to stay. Gazing up at the ceiling, he tried to figure out the room's size. He'd moved, he realized now, from a spacious place to a small one. The homes and other places must, he thought, be short of space, and that surely must make people feel depressed. You'd need to open up your heart, be endlessly patient and tolerant, if you wanted to escape the feeling.

There were four people at the dinner table: Saad, John and Mary who owned the place, and Henry, an old man, retired and into his eighties. Henry had rented the room next to Saad's, and he was the happiest to see him arrive.

The family didn't have a bad standard of living. John worked as an accountant in a company, and Mary had a job at a small clothing factory. They had two children and a very spoiled dog.

Mary was an active woman, with a nervous expression. She talked a lot and didn't hesitate to swear when necessary. She never got tired of talking, even to the dog Polly, whom she loved devotedly and always talked to nicely. She'd take her for walks every day, whether it was raining or snowing or freezing cold.

When Polly fell sick, Mary took the dog to the vet three times, and even asked a friend to bring her own dog, Cutey, to keep Polly company. Mary was a very well-organized woman, even so, a good housewife and a good cook too. Saad found their food strange and hard to eat at first, but in time he got used to it.

John, for his part, was quiet and reserved, a man of few words. He spent most of his time watching TV and reading the newspaper. On Saturday nights he'd go to the pub and come back dead drunk, to be met by Mary's scolding and shouting and the barking of the dog. He'd say not a word, while old Henry would simply say: "It's only in this house I ever saw a mule and a monkey living together."

In time a close and warm friendship sprang up between Saad and Henry, who was kind-hearted and had a strong sense of humor. Mary hated his jokes, but he always made it up to her, telling her how beautiful she was and how she was God's gift to her husband.

As time went by their friendship grew stronger. Saad would tell Henry about his family and show him pictures of his country and the letters he'd receive every week. He never, though, dared ask Henry about his family or his circumstances, because he'd heard it wasn't the custom in the

West to ask people about their personal lives.

Even so, Henry had told Saad about his divorce.

"Look, Saad," he'd told him, "when a man gets old, he starts looking like an old donkey, and he becomes useless and a burden. It would be much better to have him put to sleep. As for women, when they grow old, they're like an old car that's slow and unreliable, and needs a lot of petrol and spare parts. Even then it makes a constant noise and keeps belching out smoke. It's better just to pour on some petrol and burn it!"

Once Henry said to Saad:

"Look at that cat. It's the mate of an Anglo-Saxon cat that was killed by a bomb planted by the IRA. The poor cat wasn't Catholic or Protestant, and it certainly didn't belong to any political party."

Once, too, they were watching TV and saw a flock of wild buffalo with long horns fleeing from a wild lioness. When Henry saw that, he sank back and laughed helplessly; and when Saad asked him what the matter was, Henry said the sight made him think of the Arabs and Israel. He apologized to Saad later, saying it was just an old fool's joke.

Saad was happy to have Henry as a friend. He'd take the old man out to dinner at the Indian restaurant, and ask him to go for walks by the seaside. He even bought him a coat as a present, in place of Henry's old coat which, he'd say, had been handed down by his grandfather, George the First. They'd even take a train to spend a day in the capital. For his part, Henry would help Saad with his homework and correct his pronunciation, as well, of course, as keeping him amused with his sense of humor.

One evening, when Saad returned from school, he didn't find Henry sitting in the living room as usual; and, when he asked Mary about him, she just pointed to the old man's room.

Saad entered to find Henry looking very dejected. He asked him if he was ill, whether he'd like Saad to take him to the doctor. The old man just patted Saad's shoulder quietly.

"Everything's all right," he said.

After Saad had changed his clothes, he went back to Henry's room.

"Let's go to your favorite restaurant," he said.

They started walking, and Saad still found himself concerned about his friend. He asked Henry again, and the old man tried hard to look normal.

"It's nothing serious," he said, with a forced cheerfulness. "Nothing to worry about. I'll tell you all about it when we've eaten."

They sat down in their usual place, and Henry made a constant effort to keep his spirits up, though it was obvious something had upset him badly.

After they'd eaten, Saad said:

"Surely you realize how dear you are to me. Talk to me. Think of me as your son."

When Henry heard the word "son," he was deeply moved. He gazed at Saad with his eyes full of tears.

"I'm afraid," he said, "I shan't be seeing you any more after today."

Then, before Saad could say a word, he took a letter from his pocket and handed it to Saad.

Saad read as follows:

Dear Henry,
Mary and I have considered matters and decided that keeping you in our home is affecting our financial situation. As you know, the dog must be taken care of and so must the children. For the past three years you have been paying thirty pounds a week, while a more normal rate would be eighty pounds. We must therefore inform you, with regret, that we can no longer lodge you in our home. A new tenant will be arriving tomorrow. The grandchildren will miss you, of course. I'm so sorry, father.
Your son,
John.

Mohaymeed

The flock of birds sang as they flew in all different directions, spread in a kind of zigzag line over the fig and palm trees.

For an hour, right from the time of morning prayer, Mohaymeed had been trying to start the old water pump with the rounded blades, but all to no avail. This must have been his twentieth attempt, and all his strength had been used up. His body and face were covered with sweat, his heart was pounding and he was struggling to catch his breath.

"This machine's been out of order for six months now," he said to himself. "It's torn my heart and my shoulders, and made me spit blood."

Again and again Mohaymeed had complained about the machine's condition to Abu Ali, who'd simply say he was short of money and that a man should save his complaints for God. Once they'd sold the dates, he said, they'd fix the pump.

"If the palm trees stay thirsty," Mohaymeed would reply, "there won't be any dates. Then the pump's going to break down altogether."

Abu Ali, though, would just smile and pat Mohaymeed on the shoulder.

"Blessed be your strong arms, son," he'd answer. "Just be patient. Things will get better."

Several more times he tried to start the pump, but still he failed. Ahmad al-Yamani suggested lighting the filament inside it, in the hope this might set things working; and, after nearly half an hour of failed attempts, a cloud of dark smoke covered the place. At last, Mohaymeed emerged from this cloud successful, his face and clothes covered in black oil. He sat by the edge of the small pool and started to wash, while the water gushed and the ground shook beneath his feet as the pump roared and sent the water flowing. After cleaning himself up, he went to check on the pump and its air exhaust.

He called Ahmad, and they sat together under the big fig tree. He lit the gas to boil the kettle, put in two spoonfuls of tea and four of sugar, picked some green mint, which he added to the boiling tea, and finally poured the tea into glass cups. He looked admiringly at the color. "Perfect!" he said.

He poured another cup for Ahmad and sat happily listening to the sound of the pump, only to be interrupted by his companion, who decided, suddenly, to tell him how Faraj's donkey kept straying on to Rashed's farm, eating the eggplants and trampling the tomatoes and watermelons as it went along. Rashed, he said, had vowed to kill the donkey, claiming that Faraj always kept the animal tied up during the day, then let it loose at night. Faraj, though, had sworn, after morning prayer, that he knew nothing whatever about it, that he never let his donkey loose. Ahmad thought Rashed might actually carry out his threat—hadn't he, after all, killed Abu Thaar's dog the year before, when it attacked his chickens?

At that moment, Obeyd passed by with his rifle, carrying a leather bag filled with the birds he'd shot. Mohaymeed welcomed him, asking him to join them for a cup of tea, and Obeyd leaned his rifle against the tree trunk. Mohaymeed asked him for a share of the shoot. "Of course," Obeyd said. Mohaymeed hung the bag of birds on one of the branches and told Obeyd he was only joking.

"There are plenty of birds this year," he said, pouring Obeyd a second cup of tea, "but be careful where you're shooting. The trees are full of men picking the dates. Only the day before yesterday a bullet whizzed right past my head. It was shot from a long way off, thank, heaven, and it missed! The hunters have such an eye on the birds they don't see anything else."

"Don't worry," Obeyd said. "There won't be any problems."

Mohaymeed pulled the belt tight around his waist and put the rope on his right shoulder. Then he swarmed up the palm tree and started picking the dates. Twice he filled the mat beneath the tree. Later the dates would be packed into boxes and taken to market.

When the pool was filled, the water was diverted toward the clover, which hadn't been watered for the past three days. Next

Mohaymeed moved on to the cows in the barn and emptied ten buckets of water into the trough. While he was there, he spotted a snake, which he killed straight away and hung on a pomegranate tree for Abu Ali to see when he brought the lunch. Finally he gathered a huge bundle of hay and set it in front of the hungry cows.

"Do you think Rashed really will kill Faraj's donkey?" Ahmad asked.

Mohaymeed made no comment. He had countless things to do and he didn't want to discuss the matter—he generally avoided gossip anyway. Ahmad, though, went on.

"I think Rashed might do it. He's a real devil, and he hates Faraj, because he doesn't keep a proper watch on his donkey and sheep. Actually, I hope they do have a fight!"

Mohaymeed put the leather bag on his shoulder and climbed the palm tree once more, picking dates and singing for his loved ones. You would have thought the palm trees, as they swayed back and forth, were dancing to his tuneful voice.

His voice, though, started to tremble. His eyes were filled with tears and his heart with sighs. It was a year now since he'd last seen his parents, and his wife and only daughter, who was just two years old. He sang on, scanning the distant horizon, as if searching out his loved ones. But he was far away, and they were down in the south. In two months, he thought, the moment the dates were sold, he'd collect his wages and take the first car home, to receive his parents' blessings and hold his daughter in his arms.

The wind blew harder, and Mohaymeed sang on. The leather bag was filled with dates now. He was just about to move it to his right shoulder when it slipped, breaking the branch to which he was clinging. He fell, and his head struck the walls of the water pool, his blood mingling with the water and the dates.

"Mohaymeed!" Ahmad cried. "Mohaymeed!"

But Mohaymeed was just a floating body in the pool. The water pump was still pumping, while the wind blew the black smoke far away.

At the Company of Hope

"Things will never get any better." A notable saying, which will live on for many generations to come.

"I can't make a more efficient lot of employees from these ____s in a month," Abu Walid, the Director, said sarcastically. "And not in two months either, or even a year or two—especially when the youngest is nearly thirty years old and can't even write a simple letter without mistakes. How can I do my job properly when I'm surrounded by a brilliant bunch like this? If you want the company to develop and get ahead, you need to look for better employees. Till that happens, things just won't improve at all."

"I think you're quite wrong," replied Mr. Majed, the Company's inspector. "The fact is, you don't understand what human development's about. Management studies are getting more sophisticated by the day. If we don't develop our management system, we'll never develop ourselves. We need to adopt a new philosophy, one that says: 'Things can always get better.'"

Abu Walid, hearing this, had to laugh.

"Those employees you're talking about," Mr.

Majed went on, "are only human. They're sane, capable people. If you'd just trust them, just encourage them and show them what to do, the company would surge ahead.

"We've studied, in western management science, how encouraging employees, and trusting in their abilities, along with boosting their morale, will help them explore their capacities further, bring out hidden skills they're not even aware of. There'd be a major rise in productivity. The discovery of hidden talents would be positively reflected, in constant, ongoing success, leading to a startling improvement in performance."

Abu Walid began to show signs of boredom.

"Listen, Mr. Majed," he said. "Frankly, I haven't studied any of those things you've just talked about. In fact I've never even read any of them, in east or west. Maybe I'm wrong. Maybe it's not even good management. What I do know is that any science, in management or any other field, needs the right conditions if you're to put it into practice."

"What do you mean?" asked Mr. Majed.

"I mean there need to be certain basic things in place, regarding the working conditions you talked about, for your theory to work."

"Quite right," replied Mr. Majed.

"And those conditions aren't to be found with the employees of this company," pursued Abu Walid.

"That's your judgement, of course," Mr. Majed said. "Although such an opinion requires the application of certain academic criteria."

"Well, I'm not rejecting scientific procedure. And you're an expert, I know. So, go ahead! You're free to apply your theory to these employees and come up with your conclusions."

"That's exactly what I mean to do. There are a lot of employees, though. It will need a good deal of time and effort. According to my studies, the best method, in a situation like this, is to select a number of employees and make a case study. I'll apply this method and start with employee number five. Here we are:

Name: Fayez
Qualifications: Intermediate level (prep.)
Job Description: Archives Officer."

Fayez was a tall, broad-shouldered man, his thick chest hair showing through his unbuttoned robe. His sleeves were rolled up, his *ghutra* and *igal* untidy. Mr. Majed asked him a few questions he'd devised to form a preliminary study of employees' standards, then jotted down his own remarks. Fayez's answers, he noted, were clear, but lacking in depth and consistency.

"Tell me about your work, please, Fayez," Mr. Majed said. "Be frank."

"My work tires me out," he was told. "I sit on this chair from 7:30 in the morning till 2:30 in the afternoon. I never move. All I do is sort and file papers. Later on, I put the files up on the shelves. I come to work looking clean usually, and by the time I leave I look like a mortician. The worst thing is, almost everything's forbidden in this place. You can't smoke! You can't make a phone call! You can't talk! I work like a donkey. It's not a very pleasant situation, as you can see. And then Abu Walid, may God keep him, doesn't make things any easier. He shouts all day long! That's all I can think of. Do you need to know anything else or can I get back to work?"

"Thank you, Fayez," said Mr. Majed.

"Goodbye."

Employee number five left, and in came employee number seven:

Name: Nasr

Job Description: Economic Researcher.

Nasr was very short and thin, with sharp eyes that flickered constantly. He was extremely tense, as though fearful of something. The moment the Inspector started asking him about working conditions, the words came shooting out as if a radio had been switched on. He spoke at high speed, and the words weren't clear. Covering his mouth and nose with his hand, he paused to take a breath, then started talking all over again.

Mr.. Majed did his best to calm Nasr down and make him less nervous, so as to understand some of what he was trying to say (he suffered from a stammer too). But the man just gabbled even faster:

"Wo - wo - work ggggoood, but the sa - sa - salary is tootoootooo sm - sm -small. This is wrrrrr - wrrrongggg! They shshshould immm - prooooove the worrrk connn - di - di - tions!"

Abu Walid's attempts to intervene just made Nasr angry. He started waving his arms around and kicking with his legs. His face turned red, his eyes sparked and he almost fell into a fit.

The Director pulled back, while the Inspector remained completely silent. The two exchanged confused and fearful looks. Nasr was left to calm down finally, after which he got up and left the room muttering.

Employee number thirteen entered next:
Name: Mursi
Job Description: Head of Typists.

Mursi was a huge, tall man in his mid-forties. His big head was bald with just a little gray hair growing at the sides. He saluted the Inspector.

"On behalf of all my colleagues," he said, "I should like to welcome you to our company. It's truly a great honor to have an inspector visit us. I've been working for this company for six years now, and this is the first time an inspector's ever visited us.

"When I first came here, I worked as a typist. I used to type a hundred words a minute. I've suggested to the Director we should buy a computer, so as to improve standards of work. I'm an expert in computers by the way."

Mr. Majed gave him a look and went on writing down his remarks.

"Please don't forget about the computer, sir," Mursi added.

Abu Walid shot Mursi a meaning glance, and Mursi turned and left the room, wishing them goodbye.

Next it was the turn of employee number forty-three:

Name: Ibrahim
Qualifications: Preparatory Level Certificate. Failed twice in the second year.
Job Description: Technical Supervisor, Personnel Dept.

Ibrahim wasn't very tall. His face wore a stern expression, and he had a big nose and wide, blank eyes. His beard was thick and untidy. He sat down with no sign of respect or discipline.

Mr. Majed asked the same questions he'd asked the other employees. Then came the question directly concerning Ibrahim's job.

"How's your work, Ibrahim?"

"What do you mean?"

"I mean, how do you find your work?"

"You can see for yourself," Ibrahim said.

"OK, can you describe to me just what you do?" Majed asked.

"I don't understand."

"I mean, please explain your work to me."

"The Director can explain all that better than I can."

"Do you have any problems or difficulties at work?"

"No, it isn't tiring in the least."

"Do you have any suggestions for improving standards?"

"Improving standards? How do you mean?"

"What I really mean is, the branch needs some improvements. What are your views on that?"

"What does that have to do with me? If they want to improve standards, that's their business."

And with that Ibrahim casually left the room, without even saying goodbye.

Abu Walid looked at Mr. Majed.

"Well," he said sarcastically, "what do you say, Mr. Inspector? Ibrahim was recommended by Abu Ahmad, who's on the Board of Directors. I believe he's a cousin of Abu Ahmad's wife."

Majed looked at the list of employees and called for number twenty-nine:

Name: Assad

Qualifications: Poultry Nutritionist

Job Description: Accountant.

Assad was nearly forty years old, with a gingery-colored face, blue eyes and blond hair. He was chubby, quite short and had a thick neck. He smiled as he stood in front of the Inspector, gazing down at the ground.

"At your service, sir!" he said.

Then, before Mr. Majed could even finish asking his questions, he replied:

"I'm Assad, I have a Diploma in Poultry Nutrition. I'm good, sir. I keep good records of the accounts, and I work day and night to do a good job. I'm doing all I can for the company's welfare. If you wish, sir, I could show you the account books, the invoices and the expenditure vouchers. Everything is a hundred per cent correct."

Taking a deep breath, the Inspector tapped the desk with his fingers. He would, he announced, interview employee number fifty, and that would be the last.

Abdul Rahman, also known as "Abu Khaled," entered the room. He was over fifty years old, and Mr. Majed was impressed by his appearance. He looked very neat in his white robe and black *bisht*, and he was carrying an expensive turquoise rosary. He had a round face, a black beard—most probably dyed—and was wearing perfume.

He entered and welcomed the Inspector with a smile. Then, when he reached the Inspector, he began reciting lines of poetry. Mr. Majed asked him to stop, saying he had some questions he'd like him to answer.

"Before you ask me anything," Abdul Rahman said, "please allow me to invite you to dinner at my home tonight. Don't refuse, or you'll force me to say the word 'resignation!'"

The Inspector was confused, not knowing how to react. He hadn't expected anything like this. Abu Walid instantly intervened.

"All right, Abu Khaled," he said. "We'll do as you ask. But first, please sit down and answer the Inspector's questions."

Abdul Rahman sat down and answered the Inspector's inquiry about the nature of his work.

"I'm the company poet," he told him. "Work's going well enough. Whenever there's a special occasion at the company, I write a poem or two. I read one for the beginning of the event and one for the end. The people in the company have no complaints about my work. As for outside work, that's good too, thanks be to God. Nowadays, sir, poetry's better than salaries or stocks and shares. I sell it for a thousand a line, two or three thousand sometimes, depending on the buyer."

Abdul Rahman, so Abu Walid told the Inspector later, had been recommended by the Director-General of the Parent Company. He'd been hired as an adviser.

That evening, Mr. Majed lay in his bed reflecting on what he'd seen and heard. He'd been briefed to write an urgent official report dealing with the poor performance at this branch of the company, which he was to present to the Board of Directors next morning at an emergency meeting called to consider the issue. How, he wondered, should he start, and what should he write?

The night passed, and still he hadn't been able to write a word. And it was just the same when he sat down at his desk next morning. Finally, he entered the conference room with nothing written at all. He had no idea where to start, and certainly no idea where to end.

As the meeting was about to begin, he looked at the file he was supposed to have prepared. He felt nervous. He'd been briefed to carry out this official mission and he had to be truthful. He always told the truth whatever the situation, never compromising in the matter. And yet, if he told the truth here, many of the employees would be adversely affected; even some of the board members would be harmed. Should he try to find some compromise?

Finally, he decided to explain the whole situation, come what may. As the President of the company opened the meeting, Majed's face turned red and he started breathing heavily. They were very difficult moments. His heart was pounding and he felt exhausted.

The members listened attentively as the President talked on, while Majed tried nervously to concentrate on what was being said. The

President proudly described the ideal management development the company had achieved in conjunction with its branches, and spoke of the high level of competence among the employees.

The minutes passed, and still no one asked Mr. Majed anything or even tried to discuss any issue with him. He began to relax, though he felt some pain at the base of his back.

The meeting lasted for two hours and ended with everyone clapping. To his astonishment, Mr. Majed found himself clapping too.

Sabeh al-Layl

The caravan struggled on through the storm, fighting against the fierce wind. The frightened travellers knew there was nothing they could do, in the doomed, dark night, but await their destiny in this ocean of thirst and silence, of sand and mirage.

The storm covered their faces with sand, as the desert grew ever wider, leaving only the mirage to play its game of deception. The tracks, harsh and difficult, cut the camels' feet, and the men's weary eyes spoke eloquently of their fatigue and hardship.

The desert as vast as ever—the open skies—and the endless road. The travellers lost in their fears and uncertainty.

Sabeh al-Layl was the sole visionary among the travellers. His burning eyes saw only a calm oasis amid the pitch darkness. He was hopeful, with a heart full of confidence and trust, a soul that refused to know despair. He was the only traveler who felt able to sing in this fearful sea of death. He believed men's strong will could defeat death and illusion; that it could defeat the desert, shorten all distances and paths. The voice of the woman taken prisoner cried out within him, as if challenging death itself.

He was a young man, with a brave heart and sharp-looking eyes that shone on through the storm and darkness. The caravan came to a halt, and the travelers rested after a long and exhausting haul.

He was a tall Arab knight that the desert had tanned. Within him was a wild call, like that of a hungry wolf howling for aid. Only he among the travellers could hear the young woman's voice crossing the desert, and the storm and the mirage, to nestle deep in his soul. His heart, his soul, heard only the cries and pleas of the chained prisoner, whose flesh was torn from lashing and whose face was scarred by the nails of hatred.

He stood like a hungry wolf awaiting its prey. He struck the ground with his stick, repeatedly, hoping to break this sea of sand; but, alas, his stick had no power to work miracles.

The messages were borne to him on the wind, from every side. He listened, read, wrote, inquired, thought, planned, woke, not knowing which path to follow.

His anguish grew stronger with each night that passed. Days, months, years even passed, as he fought down his sorrow and swallowed his pain. Still he sought some way out, for the right moment to come, but all roads were blocked and hard to cross. No road would ever give security to the traveller.

With a hawk's boldness, he would saddle his

Sabeh al-Layl

horse, make ready his spears; but the night would fall and break the hawk's wings, leaving him awaiting still another dawn, his eyes open wide.

Sabeh al-Layl would seek adventure amid the spreading mirage and the desert storms. The rocks and sands burned in the heat, and the trees turned to dry branches and leaves, as if the sun had plunged down on the earth.

Scattered tents—thin horses—gaunt camels—lean faces with weary eyes. Only Sabeh al-Layl had those sharp eyes that strove for victory. Could victory dwell amid such wretchedness? What victory could come from these worn out travellers? A tiger will first banish every fear, before falling on its prey. Sabeh al-Layl was resolved and ready to attack.

For all her despair, her face shone like the dawn. She laughed as she let her hair hang loose, and danced. "She must have lost her wits," the guard thought.

She watched, with all her senses, as her knight crossed the desert on his white horse. Her eyes pierced the prison's thick walls and the dark veil of the night. She saw him as he approached. She prepared for her wedding night, with a flooding joy only the desert itself could contain.

The moment came.

The chains were tight, the eyes open wide, the walls of the fortress all ears. The rifles were ready to fire out bullets of death. The hearts were pounding, the muscles tensed.

A dim light—dates—milk—prayers—death—fingers on the triggers—fists clutching swords and spears. The night was slow and plodding, and the men could hear their own heavy breath.

Death encompassed everything. The men in the fortress listened hard. The heavy chains—the wild adventure—the courage—the madness. Nothing mattered any longer. Fate appeared clouded, death inevitable, should those weary feet and exhausted souls tremble for a moment.

The light came from the East. The lion attacked—roared. The narrow alleyways widened and all distances vanished—fire broke out in the fortress—cries—flame shooting.

Sabeh al-Layl attacked—he lunged out and roared. The prey fell. The small door opened, and all barriers broke together with the maiden's chains. A slain body was dragged, like a slaughtered lamb, before the palace gate.

The sound of song and the beating of drums rang out through the desert, reaching every town and village. The earth shook with fervor and the swords glowed.

Sabeh al-Layl was marrying the beautiful maiden.

Editor-in-Chief

Strolling lazily into his office, Amer told his secretary not to transfer any calls or show anyone in. He sat in his chair stretching, yawning, twisting his head left and right, his arms resting on the desk. Then he started rubbing his eyes and, as his body slid down the chair, began once more to stretch his arms and legs. Finally, he put his arms back on the table and nestled his head between his hands.

This was his usual way of acting when he got to his office early—before one in the afternoon, that is. The secretary was well enough acquainted with his mood and the way he liked to start his working day. It usually took him half an hour to warm up, before he could act normally.

He told the secretary to bring his coffee, and, as she walked in with the tray, he gave her a strange look that made her feel uneasy. She tried, with a nervous gesture, to straighten her hair and dress, then hurried out to fetch the folders; but he stopped her.

He lit his pipe and sipped his cup of coffee with enjoyment, watching the smoke drift slowly up into the ceiling. Then he asked for a second cup of coffee, which helped him wake up finally.

"Hind's on the line," said the secretary.

"Get her off," he said.

"It's Hind," the secretary repeated.

"Get her off, I tell you!" came the reply.

She shrugged her shoulders. "Things are really changing!" she thought, as she walked out.

The Editor-in-Chief called his secretary back and asked if she had a tape recorder. The request surprised her. Surely, she said, the editors must have one.

"No," he replied. "What the editors have isn't good enough. Bring me a big one."

The music blared out and the song had him on his feet and dancing. The secretary hurried out of the office and closed the door behind her, but he shouted to her to keep the door wide open. As the sound of the music reached the nearby offices, the employees stopped their work to listen, and some, in their curiosity, stuck their heads out to see what was going on. Even Lamia, one of the clerks, thrust her head out with the others, hard enough for her hair band to fall off, making her bushy dyed hair stick out.

The Editor-in-Chief played the song again, only louder this time, and started singing along with it, till his voice actually began to drown out the singer. No one dared ask any questions, but everyone was looking and listening, wondering what was going on. He must have gone crazy, they thought, or else he was still recovering from the night before.

The recorder stopped playing at last, and the heads disappeared amid astonishment and disbelief. He called his secretary and handed her the tape.

"Make three copies of this," he said. "It's a present from Judi." She nodded. "Is my editorial ready?" he asked, as she hurried out.

"No, the editor hasn't sent it yet."

"Tell him to hurry up!"

A few moments later she returned.

"Editor Attieh's sick," she told him. "Your editorial hasn't been done."

"Sick?" he yelled furiously. "Sick, did you say? Well, that's not my fault. Tell him to come in straight away. Either that or send someone to pick him up."

When the secretary came back, she told him, uneasily, that Attieh had a severe headache with fever. The doctor had said he should stay in bed.

"What are we going to do then?" the editor exploded. "We can't bring the issue out without an editorial. It's ridiculous!"

"Quite absurd," she agreed "Suppose we ask Salah to write it instead?"

He started yelling all over again. "Don't be stupid. That's a ridiculous suggestion! Salah's wordy, he isn't a fit person to write the editorial. It's all your fault. You should have told Attieh to write some extra editorials, to keep up his sleeve for emergencies like this."

"But you never told me to," she replied.

"Do I have to tell you everything? You're the secretary. You're supposed to be ready when things like this happen. Call Abdul Salam at the *Golden Daily* magazine."

"Abdul Salam's abroad. Covering that conference—on Fighting Illiteracy in the Third World."

"Then call Siraj al-Din at the *Tawabir* paper."

"Siraj al-Din's been taken to hospital. For an appendix operation."

"All right then, call Attieh and tell him to dictate the editorial to you, over the phone."

"But he has a high fever."

"Didn't you hear what I said? Have him dictate the editorial over the phone!"

A short while later she returned and handed him the editorial. The Editor-in-Chief started reading.

"'Curse this world,'" he read. "'And curse writers! What are writers but slaves anyway, and what are all these magazines and newspapers but spider's webs filled with flies and pigs and worms? Oh writing, forgive me, please. Oh pen, excuse, please, my savage way of talking. I'm drowning in a sewer of madness! Curse this fever. I've started raving.'"

The Editor-in-Chief shrieked at the top of his voice.

"Son of a bitch! Did Attieh come out with this stuff?" He started tearing at his hair. "All these years I've seen him as a trusted assistant. And now, out of the blue, all this bile comes pouring out." He went on yelling, beside himself. "Dear God! What am I to do with these malignant people?"

It was the first time she'd ever heard him mention the name of God. He actually called to mind her dead mother, who, if irritated by her or one of her sisters, would say: "Oh God, where can I go, what can I do?"

"No, no," she said quietly. "No, he must just be raving. It must be the fever."

"Get me any of the animals on this newspaper," he shouted. "Any one of them that can write an editorial. We can't let the issue go out without an editorial!"

She became confused. Which of the humans or animals on the paper was, she wondered, capable of writing the editorial?

"Leave it with me," she said.

He sat there, staring at her, cursing her silently. He even thought of calling her back into his office to give her a piece of his mind. Luckily she'd already left by then.

After a brief interval she walked back in and placed the editorial on his desk. He started reading, then leaped from his chair.

"This is great," he cried. "Fantastic! What genius wrote this?"

"You like it," she replied. "That's all that matters."

"No, I must know. Tell me who wrote it."

"Do you really like the piece?" she said. "Do you really think whoever wrote it is a genius?"

"Yes, yes, stop beating about the bush, will you? Tell me who this brilliant person is."

"Just me sir," she replied quietly.

Hassan's Theory

Dr. Mansour, his lecture just over, wiped the sweat from his brow and placed his spectacles on top of the pile of papers on his desk.

"Teaching," he said. "What a weary, loathsome business it is!"

"That's new coming from you," Dr. Suleyman observed. "I thought you set a lot of store by teaching."

"I did, but I'm starting to have second thoughts. The students nearly tore me to shreds today. When I was trying to explain Darwin's theory."

There was silence for a time. Dr. Suleyman was busy marking exam scripts, while Dr. Mansour elected to rest his mind. Dr. Usman, meanwhile, said nothing, looking out of the big window at the clear blue skies.

Dr. Hassan came into the room, whistling a tune from an old song.

"Good morning, my dear doctors!" he said. "Why all these grave looks? Tell me, Dr. Mansour, has some disaster struck the USA and Russia, or the bakery next door maybe?"

Still whistling, he opened his briefcase, took out a sandwich he'd just bought and started eating.

"What's the matter with you all today?" he asked, having finished his first mouthful. "You look like a bunch of old people at a funeral."

Dr. Suleyman, laughing at the notion, picked up his glasses and pen.

"It's Dr. Mansour," he said.

"What's wrong with him?"

"The students almost tore him apart."

"What a tasty prey he would have made," Dr. Hassan remarked. Dr. Mansour was fat, though still quite young.

Dr. Mansour looked at Dr. Hassan.

"It's beyond me," he said, "how you can eat a whole pot of cooked beans for breakfast, plus all those sandwiches you keep munching between classes, and still be as thin as if you were starving in Africa."

Dr. Hassan smiled, still chewing on his sandwich.

"I come," he said, "from a family where no one's ever weighed more than sixty kilos. They never would, even if they tried to eat the whales in the sea. I'll never get chubby and plump, don't worry."

"You must come from a family of lizards," Dr. Mansour joked.

"To get back to the original subject," Dr. Suleyman said, "why are you so fed up with your students?"

Everyone laughed. Dr. Hassan broke in.

"Let's be serious," he said. "Hasn't Darwin's

theory aroused a good deal of controversy in scientific circles? And started losing its influence?"

"It's only a theory," Dr. Mansour replied, "based on certain experiments that were never completed. As such, it's never been proved true, or completely rejected either. That's why it's still open to debate."

"I've been mulling over a different theory," Dr. Hassan pursued, "the complete opposite to Darwin's. I've been reluctant to discuss it, though, for fear of the anger, and the false accusations, I'd get in return."

They all stared at him in amazement.

"What kind of theory?" they asked.

"It's called the theory of decline and retardation," Dr. Hassan explained. "The complete contrary, in other words, of Darwin's theory of evolution. This theory states that human beings were first created in a perfect form—as all the religions claim they were—and that industrial growth and development, stemming from the collected knowledge and experiments of mankind, have led to our present civilization. As such, it's not a matter of humans nowadays being more complete and perfect than they were long ago. On the contrary, humans today are more reckless and lacking in wisdom, with a tendency to strive to destroy themselves. I have compelling evidence for this."

"Such as?" Dr. Suleyman asked.

"Well, take the creatures that became extinct. Dinosaurs, for instance, which developed gradually into crocodiles and ended as lizards.

Or donkeys, which come from the same line as horses, or cats which come from lions."

"Your theory would need plenty of research done on it!" Dr. Usman observed.

Dr. Hassan continued.

"The same applies to plants. Scientists have found that some plants, such as apples, figs and grapes, have grown weaker over the years. They no longer taste as they once did, and they're getting smaller, with their taste changing in the process."

Dr. Mansour, laughing, said that apples nowadays tasted just like lotus fruit.

"We see plenty of things deteriorating drastically," Dr. Hassan pursued. "And by this argument the ape must once have been a human being. Perhaps some feckless people, who couldn't adapt to harsh conditions, or fight wars, decided to live with the animals. And so they adopted their way of life and gradually turned into apes."

"Are you serious about this, Dr. Hassan?" Dr. Suleyman asked.

"I can't say I'm convinced," Dr. Mansour said, "but I do think you should go ahead and announce your theory. There's certainly room for debate."

"I'm afraid to," replied Dr. Hassan.

"Why?"

"Because the theory still isn't complete."

"In what way?" they asked, all together.

"Well, if I put forward the theory that man's evolution depends on the knowledge he acquires over the years, and that lack of knowledge serves to aid his decline and hence his extinction, then my fears are confirmed."

"What fears?" they asked.

"I'm afraid," he said, after a short pause, "of what will happen to the head of the Arab."

"The head of the Arab?"

"Yes. For in that case the head's bound to grow smaller because it isn't being used. As long as the Arab's incapable of defending himself and his rights, and uses force to sort out his differences, and as long as he imports matches, and darning needles, and razors for shaving, and tissues for cleaning, then he doesn't need to use his brain. And so his head, not being used, will shrink and eventually vanish. On that basis, future Arab generations will be born without brains. Just empty skulls, without eyes, or ears, or even mouths."

"Almighty God!" they said in unison.

"And as for the generations that follow those, they might be born with tails and paws. This, of course, follows from the theory of decline and retardation, which is the contrary of the theory of evolution."

Dr. Suleyman nodded in total agreement.

"After two or three generations," Dr. Hassan went on, "the Arab will become a member of the higher ape species. He'll keep the ability to dress and eat and dance—these are enduring characteristics—but he might mistakenly put the left shoe on the right foot and make a spectacle of himself. And yet he'll win great victories."

"What?" they cried.

"You see, he'll rid himself, quite naturally, of all the modern diseases, like heart attacks, strokes, high blood pressure, diabetes, ulcers, along with all the psychiatric and mental illnesses, because he's lost the ability to react. Who knows, maybe his digestive system will get to be like an ox's, only less sensitive."

"If what this man's saying does come true," Dr. Usman remarked, perplexed, "then we'll be in big trouble!"

The Cat

There was once a wealthy lady who lived in a mansion and owned a beautiful cat, with which she played, ate, and even slept. The people who worked in the mansion loved this cat, and little by little they grew to respect it and finally to fear it.

One day an alley cat entered the mansion, and the lady's cat grew very fond of him. A week later, though, he went off, leaving the aristocratic cat wailing, miaowing and searching for him.

Everyone looked for the runaway cat, through all the houses and streets and alleys, but to no avail. Even the mayor offered a generous reward to anyone who would bring the cat alive. But the alley cat had vanished, leaving the wealthy lady's cat sad along with her mistress. Many other cats resembling the beloved one were brought to the sad cat, but, each time, she'd sniff them then start to scratch them.

The wealthy lady, beginning to panic now, summoned various vets to help cure the poor cat, but they all failed. Even psychiatrists were called in, but the case remained hopeless.

The cat, meanwhile, grew so weak she could no longer walk properly. One day she left the mansion and went to stand in the middle of the road. The traffic policeman stopped the cars, while the cat stood there staring at the people, till at last they became annoyed and the children, tired of sitting in the cars in the heat, started crying. One of the drivers became so angry he blew his horn, and the policeman arrested him.

The wealthy lady, whose mansion stood in one of the most prominent streets in the city of Arboush, looked out and saw her cat staring at the cars. The sight of her cat made her very happy, and she started waving to it.

Just at that moment an eagle came and snatched the cat, then soared up high into the sky. The wealthy lady went running out, screaming and pleading for help, but the eagle was long gone. Some time later, a black dot was seen falling from the sky, then hitting the ground at high speed. The cat was transformed into scattered flesh and blood.

The wealthy lady picked up the remains of her precious cat, then yelled at the people:

"You killed my cat! You killed my cat!"

In the meantime an officer had arrested a poor man carrying a bag with a cat inside. The officer asked the lady if this was the cat she'd been looking for, and she cried out:

"That's the cat! That's the cat!"

She told the policeman to kill the man who'd been behind the death of her cat. But the poor man said:

"This is no cat, my lady. This is a lion."

"Are you telling me that's a lion, you brute?" the lady shouted back.

"Yes, my lady," thfe poor man replied. "In this city the lions have turned into cats!"

The Tin Can

The waves broke angrily on the shore as he trudged along, nursing the rage that blazed inside him. Ever since he'd started his new job, with this fearful boss of his, he'd been striving not to complain, to endure the situation somehow; but now he couldn't bear it any longer. According to the laws of nature everything changes, but that didn't seem to apply to his demented boss.

A rusty tin can, half eaten away by the salt and sand, caught his eye. He stood there looking at it, with a good deal of attention and concern. Why he'd been so suddenly drawn to the can he couldn't say. He looked at the bottom, which was torn and riddled with holes, while the upper part had turned to a rusty brown from exposure to the sun and moisture. He found himself totally entranced by the can; he couldn't take his eyes off it, as though it were some work of art. What, he wondered, was wrong with him? It was only a rusty old can. He went up and walked around it, scrutinizing its smallest detail. He counted the holes, checking on the size of each one and even studying their shapes. Then he got down on the sand and peered at the gaping spaces through which the sunlight poured.

He even noticed the can hadn't been opened, though someone must have tried to open it not too long before. For a while he felt the urge to touch it, but he was afraid he might damage it, on account of the state it was in, and so lose the wonderful feeling it had given him. He wished he could stay longer with the can, never part with it. He felt a kinship with the rusty body, his mind and will quite captivated by the clumsy sight it presented.

He wanted to take the can back with him to the city. But he was afraid that, if he moved it, it would fall apart and lose its effect. Finally he decided to dig around it and take the can along with the surrounding sand. After much delicate work he managed this, and off he went to the city. He couldn't sleep that night, overwhelmed by the treasure he'd just found.

Next morning, very early, he put the sand and the tin can in his car and headed for his office, before any of the other employees, or his boss, had arrived. He placed his treasure on the boss's desk.

The Director stared hard at the can, then asked disapprovingly:

"What's this?"

"Look at it carefully," he replied. "The answer might come to you, sir."

The Director, hardly able to believe what he'd just seen and heard, took a second look, but he couldn't guess.

He drew closer to his boss without a tremor, then told him:

"It's you, sir!"

Setting Out

"Shall I leave the village? How can I?" These were the questions echoing in Abu Salem's head as he washed the animal blood from his hands. "Shall I leave the farm, the wide open spaces, the men's gatherings, and go off to the city where everybody's a nobody? Can I leave my home and neighbors? I kept saying I'd leave the village, every time I was upset by something someone said, but it was only a threat—I never really meant to do it. Has the time come at last, when I'm left with no other choice?"

Ever since his brother had persuaded him to set off and move to Riyadh, he'd had these conflicting emotions, felt this heavy load on his chest. He was happy enough to go to the new world and all the temptations awaiting him there. It would make the village people respect him; they'd talk about him just as they did about his brother Dahman.

And yet there was that other feeling, of deep melancholy, which swept through him whenever he thought of leaving the village, with its people, and good friends, and childhood memories. This feeling was, he realized now, overwhelming, and he wished his brother had never told him how he'd found a job for him in the big city, how he should leave as soon as he could.

Abu Salem left the animal yard, where he'd hung the slaughtered sheep, and returned home to where Um Salem was standing with her hands on her head, pretending to watch the pigeons on the fence that separated their house from their neighbors'. In reality she was listening to a painful question she didn't like to hear or answer. "Are we really leaving our home?" She must have suffered the most from pondering just what such a decision would mean.

Her thoughts, though, were cut short by Abu Salem's sudden appearance.

"Um Salem," he said. And silence followed.

She sensed well enough what was going on in his mind; but, instead of talking, they just exchanged looks that conveyed exactly what each of them felt. Then he asked her where their son Salem was, because he wanted Salem to go and invite the top village people to the dinner held in honor of his brother.

Salem was the only one happy with the news. He'd heard his cousin describe Riyadh and the incredible things they had there, things Salem couldn't even begin to imagine. His cousin, who was inclined to exaggerate, had talked of their big villa with trees around it. Tomorrow, Salem thought, he'd tell his friends how he too would be leaving the village, with all its dogs and donkeys, and they'd envy him for going away.

Abu Salem gazed at his fellow villagers who'd gathered to attend the dinner.

"You all know," he told them, "how precious your faces are to me, how I see you all as part of my family. You're my people, and the village is my home. In fact each house in the village is my home, and each one of you is my brother." As he said the word "brother," he almost choked. He sighed, then went on, his eyes filled with tears. "I swear, by God, that you're my people and brothers!" He went on to tell his guests of his decision to leave the village, and to set out for the city where his brother Dahman had found him a job.

Dahman had first been hired as a driver for one of the companies, then, later, he'd been promoted to the post of supervisor, before finally becoming responsible for the company's car park. It was then that he'd found his brother Salem a job as a gatekeeper there.

The village people looked angrily at Dahman. First he'd left the village himself, and now he was taking away his brother, a man they regarded as their brave protector. But Dahman had persuaded his brother to go to Riyadh, to a new world more suitable, he said, for Abu Salem and his children. He'd persuaded him that staying on in his ancestors' village would be mere waste. Abu Salem had been dazzled by his brother's talk of the future for his children, and of how his son Salem, if he stayed, would just become like many of the village's lazy animals.

That night neither Abu Salem nor his wife slept. She was kept awake by thoughts in which sadness and fear, regret and sorrow, were mingled. At dawn the people gathered around the big truck that had just arrived from the north and was heading for Riyadh. Abu Salem carried his baggage alone. No one offered to help him. They simply stood there gazing at him, with sad, tearful eyes.

Back at home, the women gathered and wept as they bade farewell to Um Salem. Even those who were jealous of her were afraid to lose her. Before leaving the house, Um Salem took one last look at her goats, then broke down in tears. Abu Salem tried to console her, but she wouldn't budge, refusing to leave the house without her goats. There was no time to argue. Abu Salem put the baby goat on his shoulder, while the rest of the animals followed him.

Before the truck set off on its journey, Um Salem thrust her head out of the back and the women took one last look at her together with her goats. As for Salem, he sat there in the truck, astonished by the many thoughts racing through his head. But he never thought he'd be writing this story in his office in a hospital in the north of Scotland, where he was studying for his doctorate.

His small head must surely have been packed with thoughts as the truck pulled off, leaving a storm of dust and tears in its wake.

The Committee

There was once a man who bought a donkey and found, afterwards, that he'd been cheated. The beast was stupid.

He went to the judge, and the judge in turn summoned the vendor, who told him he'd had little experience with donkeys. If, he went on, the judge could show the donkey lacked intelligence, then he'd return the money. Otherwise the sale should remain valid. Finally the judge, after a good deal of thought, chose to form a committee which would decide whether the donkey was stupid or not.

The committee looked thoroughly into the donkey's case. Several sessions were held, but the members only argued among themselves, and a lot of money was spent. The chairman thought it necessary to summon the vendor before the committee, and the vendor's testimony covered the donkey's family tree, behavior, preferences and date of birth. Still, though, the committee couldn't reach a verdict, and the man who'd bought the donkey was growing tired of taking the beast back and forth each morning to attend the meetings.

The Committee

At last the committee submitted a proposal to the parties concerned, who gave it their full approval—except that the buyer objected to one feature. If, he said, just a single vet was called on, as proposed, to give the donkey a check-up, the opinion of that one vet might not come down on his side of the question. He asked, accordingly, that a committee of vets be set up to run the checks. Even then, though, the vets disagreed among themselves and couldn't reach a unanimous verdict. The check-ups were repeated, but failed to bring the desired result.

Word of the case reached the news agencies and press, who had a field day, publishing a picture of the donkey on their front pages. Soon everyone knew about the donkey. Many of the journalists took the buyer's side, and they launched a campaign against fraud. This kind of thing, they maintained, smacked of corruption, and they warned of the evil effects on society, and of how it would put honest dealing and mutual trust in jeopardy. One young journalist, who covered the case especially well, was promoted to be Chief Editor.

People began to take a close interest in the case, which now eclipsed all other stories. They were divided, some supporting the buyer and others the vendor, who couldn't, they said, be blamed for the donkey's lack of intelligence. Meanwhile, newspaper sales reached an all-time peak—you couldn't find one after nine in the morning. The intellectuals got involved too, and started reading books about donkeys, notably

Jahiz's *Animals*.[7] As for Tawfiq al-Hakim's book, it sold right out and people had to buy photocopies.[8]

The buyer grew very tired of it all. He was spending most of his time taking the donkey from the vet's clinic to the stable, and he even had to borrow money to pay for the medical tests, and the food and transportation. Finally he went to the judge, explaining that he was tired out and needed a quick solution. The time had come, the judge realized, for the police to be called in, and so the case was referred to them; and they, after due consideration, told the judge there were two possible solutions. The first was to send all the medical records abroad for final arbitration; the second that one of the parties to the dispute should back down. The judge rejoiced at this, applauding the wisdom of the decision.

He summoned the two parties accordingly, to attend what he supposed would be the final session. By this time word had reached the press and news agencies, who gathered outside the courtroom, together with all the other people who'd come to hear the verdict.

The judge informed both parties of the police decision and told them they must choose. The two said nothing for a time; then the vendor asked if he might see the donkey. The judge agreed to this and instructed that the beast be brought in. The vendor looked at the donkey, then, seeing how much heavier and stronger it had grown over the past months, told the judge he'd take it back and return the money. The judge, in his relief, leaped from his seat and hugged the buyer. People couldn't believe it—that the vendor had actually agreed to take the donkey back and refund the money.

Vendor and donkey walked from the courtroom to the applause of the people, to where hundreds of flashing cameras awaited them. At that the vendor whispered in his donkey's ear.

"Welcome back, my dear donkey," he said. "I swear you're the only sane creature in this town!"

Tears in the Darkness

He poured the strong tea sitting there at his desk. The tag of the tea bag was half burned and the teapot blackened from the fire. He put two spoonfuls of sugar in his cup. In the old days he'd drunk his tea without sugar—occasionally he'd used saccharin. Now, though, none of that seemed to matter.

After finishing the first cup, he felt hungry. He hadn't left the room—this room he'd arranged as his private den when he first moved into the house—since morning. He was sorting out his papers, dividing them into three groups. The first group, the papers he considered useful, went into his briefcase. The second group, made up of bills and debit notes, was burned. As for the third, unable to decide what to do with it, he just put it on his desk next to the phone, which he'd disconnected earlier that day, so as to be able to concentrate on his work.

Should he reconnect it? Checking the time, he decided his older sister must be asleep along with her children. As for his friends—so what? He dismissed them from his mind.

On the wall opposite was a picture that had often made him feel very proud, taken of him and a group of businessmen when visiting an Arab country. There he stood among the rest, with his middling-sized body and distinguished air. They were attending a dinner held in honor of the first successful deal he'd concluded, which had been a turning point in his professional life. Recalling the time and the circumstances, he sighed deeply and covered his eyes with his hands. Then he went back to drinking his tea, which was cold and bitter by now.

Getting up from his chair, he walked over to the picture, gazed at himself and smiled. Then, as his eye fixed on the secretary, he shook his head, feeling a surge of annoyance. She was pleasant and attractive, but he'd never liked her; he'd never known or tried to work out why. On the wall, too, was his certificate, in a gilded frame. He thought of throwing that in the bin too and burning it. It had never been any use to him, or brought him any benefit—it was mere living witness of those sixteen years he'd spent at school amid the scolding of his teachers and the horrors of exams. Finally, he opted not to burn it. He was too tired now to think of the things around him.

Back at his desk, among the scattered papers, he felt so hungry he wished his diary and penholder would turn to bread so he could dip them in the bitter tea! From his window he could see the fresh bread, cheese, eggs, apples, and other fruit and vegetables so beautifully displayed in the grocer's across from his house. There was no money in his pocket. He looked for some but could only find his check book. His bank account had been enormous once, so much so that his bank manager would rush out to meet him whenever he went to the place. Now it was just a flat, round circle.

He wrote out a check, for a huge amount, and carelessly signed it. In the past his signature had been famous and respected. Now it looked like a dead worm.

Just being alive brought him some comfort, reminded him life was made of profit and loss, triumph and defeat. Even so, what faced him was more than defeat—from that he could have started out again. In reality he was on the brink of ruin.

He could find no good reason for coming to such a sorry pass. Wishing just to protect his profits, he'd ventured all his money. But others had been far stronger than he was, and hadn't wanted him in their territory. He'd been too naive to stay away from those great sharks and the dangerous waters they lived in. He'd started competing with them, and they'd exploited his ignorance, pushed him to bid for tenders he was bound to lose, or which would bring only meager profit if he did win. He'd struggled on, losing three times for each time he profited. The pattern became established, and his debts and overdraft kept on growing. He'd tried to salvage what he could, to provide a decent life for himself and his family; but he'd failed. His house, or mansion rather, three stories high, had cost him millions to build; now it was owned by the bank and the three stories were vacant. His wife had moved in with her parents, along with the children. The expensive furniture and carpets had all been sold. There was nothing left but his desk and the loads of papers he was sorting out before the bank seized the house the very next morning.

Such a cruel, desolate feeling! His heart couldn't bear the bitterness of losing his own home, his children's rooms and all the memories. His eyes filled with tears.

Feeling hungry again, he searched through his pockets once more, but found nothing to buy himself a piece of bread. He strove to ignore the pangs, but couldn't. Going through the drawers of his desk, he found only papers, stamps, photos, other worthless items. Then, opening the small top drawer, he found a gold pen.

How could he have forgotten that? A close friend had made him a gift of the pen more than twenty years before, to mark the very success that made him forget all those good friends completely. He held the pen, then lifted it to his lips and placed a kiss on it.

A sense of guilt swept through him, as if the pen was exacting the harshest of revenges. Why do we forget about the beautiful things in our lives? And why do we remember them so vividly when we come across them once more? How, anyway, could we recall all those things? And why do they come to torment us?

He thought of calling his old friend, now, after twenty years, to say hello. But would the friend even recognize his voice? And could he summon up the courage to talk to him? Where would he find his friend anyway? And what did he look like now? What had become of him? How sad it was, that a person should recoil from facing close friends. That was loss indeed.

Putting the pen in his pocket, he walked down the stairs, passing through the empty corridors and halls. The shadow of a cat, reflected on the bare walls, looked like a camel's. It was the cat his daughter used to play with. Memories haunted him, passing swiftly before his eyes. He hurried out of the house, and there was a new challenge facing him. Standing in front of the grocer, he said: "I'd like some bread, cheese, and two apples."

The grocer fetched the things and put them in a bag. "I'll pay you tomorrow," he told him. But the grocer took the bag back. "No credit," he said. He tried to persuade the grocer, but the man insisted on having his money there and then.

He took out his check book, but the grocer just laughed.

"A check for a bit of bread," he said. "Good God!"

Thinking hard, he touched the gold pen in his pocket, and thought: "this is my last resort." He took the pen and gazed at it as it glittered in the light. He was about to give it to the grocer, when he heard a voice inside him, screaming: "NO—" He returned the pen to his pocket and walked back home. He'd been about, he reflected, to do the stupidest thing of his life.

"Perhaps," he said, "I could make a new start with this pen."

Lying down on the bed in his den, he felt like

weeping, but couldn't shed a tear. He tried to remember the last time he'd cried, but failed. He hadn't, apparently, cried since he was a child—the only tears to come into his eyes had been tears of laughter.

Misery was a feeling so hard it could block the ducts of your tears. How useless he felt! Curling up in his bed, he fell asleep at last, and, in his dream, saw his mother setting him on her lap and stroking his hair, while he sucked at her milk that tasted like honey. He woke, feeling happy now, and not hungry any more. He tried to see his mother and found only darkness. Then it was that he broke down in tears, but only to drown in a darkness without end.

Flocks of Doves

As she sat in her beautiful room, there came to her mind the love story of Fatima bint al-Munzer. She'd fallen in love with a handsome poet, who'd secretly visit her quarters in the palace, smuggled in by her chambermaid. The servants and the rest of the household had wondered about that heavy load the chambermaid carried, each night, to the princess's room! She tried to relive the moments of the famous story, tried even to sing, but her voice was choked off by the marble, and the mirrors and paintings, of her own palace.

She was, just like Fatima, a princess in her palace, except that she didn't of course have any official title. She had authority over anything and anybody, except herself.

Lassitude, weariness, depression—all these sprang from the loneliness and boredom lording it over her. She could see the flocks of doves flying freely about, flapping their wings and building their nests among the trees, while the drops from the marble fountains reflected the lovely hues of the rainbow and the butterflies danced to the sweet tunes of our mother nature. She tried playing with the locks of her hair, but managed only a deep sigh that blew the hair from her face, adding to her air of perplexity and trouble.

Away in the distance she could see a flag, hoisted on the roof of a small house—the house where she herself might have ended had fate not intervened and brought her where she was today. It was there, where the flag flew high, that she'd once had a dream.

She still remembered how, together, they'd hoisted the flag to help guide the flocks of doves. It was a special day of her youth; a day that would live forever and flourish in her memory.

She'd never forget it, how they were both sweating from the heat of that summer day. Their youthful dreams were stronger by far than any hateful separation and dispersal. Now, today, she was tasting the bitterness of confinement in this splendid glass dome. He'd suffered too, and decided at last to leave the district, shaking off the sorrow and memories. Nothing remained but the shadow of the fluttering flag, standing firm after so many years. She'd look at the flag and let her mind wander. Imagination was the only freedom left in her protected prison, and it returned her now to the princess and her handsome poet.

She was wakened from her daydream by the sound of footsteps, heralding the daily summons to lunch. The sight of all the different kinds of food, and the servants in their gaudy uniforms, always drove her to distraction. She'd sit at the table, removing her mind from the talk: shallow and repetitive, then turning, every so often, to malice and innuendo.

Silence was a great blessing. The walls, the ceilings, the columns were, she felt, drenched in all those shallow conversations. Tedium ruled, and she could beat it only through total silence; such was her chosen means of facing the meaningless world around her. She would, she decided, ignore all those newspaper stories, all that gossip. Her dream world would be her only talk, night and day. That was why she stood at her window continually, looking to a world stretching from the locks of her hair to the fluttering flag.

Sitting facing her, on the edge of their bed, he'd told her of his business coup, how he'd closed a deal of major proportion. Once he'd told her how she herself was the finest, most important deal ever to come his way. From that moment on, she'd had the feeling of being one among his many precious belongings, which he'd keep in bank vaults or in his own safe at home.

She'd realized by then how she'd lost her whole life; and how she could only face such a vast loss through loyalty and obedience. Her body, her feelings, were in a state of ceaseless conflict. He was plunged in his work and ambition, while she lived on in her lavish, secluded world, along with her silence and humming that filled the corridors and rooms of this hushed place.

Everything was conducted in utter quiet. People didn't speak, they whispered. Everything was ruled by harsh restriction, quite unlike the way things were in the annexes of the palace—

there was more life there, and less formality, as though these places lay beyond the palace laws and its way of life sharp as the blades of the gilded knives.

Everything around her was beautiful and splendid, the envy of countless other women; but she hated every part of it. She hadn't been born a cow to be grazed and milked, nor was she a gem to be locked away in a silk-lined box. The ceaseless sounds within her head, the longing that swept through every part of her when she gazed from her window, would drive her from that secure box, transform her to a question mark piercing this luxurious world of hers.

If only, she thought, they'd let her eat a simple piece of bread, enjoy the fresh air and freedom she'd known once. She found herself reciting a line from a poem, which spoke of a house with a soul being better, by far, than a palace with none. Maysoun, Fatima, Waddah, those were the true treasures of her world.[9]

As they drank their tea in the air-conditioned room, she said: "Which of the deals is worth more? Today's or me?"

The inquiry shocked and angered him; he hadn't expected a hurtful question like that, at a moment of such vibrant joy. He made an effort to govern his anger and seem at ease.

"What do you mean?" he asked, smiling.

She smiled back, then let her gaze drop. As rage welled up inside her, her hair fell onto her shoulders. The evening sun cast its light on the palm trees, and the garden was plunged in the tranquil colors of dusk. The doves rose, happily, into the skies.

"Today's deal," he told her suddenly. "It's yours! What would you like to have?"

She gazed out at the horizon.

"I wish," she said, "I could be a dove, and fly from this palm tree to that flag fluttering up there in the wind."

The Snow Siege

Snow was falling on this hill, in the north of Scotland, overlooking Loch Ness and its legendary monster. The white flakes, like cotton, covered the district round about, filling me with a sense of total enchantment. It was thrilling to feel I was in a world so utterly different from the one I was used to. It was good too, from time to time, to feel far from everything. A son of desert, sun and sand, I was astounded by this vast desert of snow.

Here in the lakeside hotel, the smell of burning logs and the fire blazing in the chimney set the blood rushing in my veins, lessening the loneliness and the effects of the spell cast on me by the snow. The logs crackled as they burned, like the sound of raindrops falling on the dry and thirsty desert.

This inn where I was staying was a very modest kind of place—and yet that was its real beauty. There was nothing extravagant, but I couldn't, either, find anything missing or wrong. In the hall, the eye was caught by a painting on the wall, showing three wolves on a snow-covered mountain. The painting looked so real—but nothing seemed to matter at that moment, apart from the warm fire.

An old man was sitting reading a newspaper, while his wife sat with her back against the armchair, enjoying the warmth of the blaze. She was dozing away, jerking back as, every so often, she tried unsuccessfully to open her eyes. It was a delightful sight: of old age making its final peace with all life's worries and hardships. In the corner opposite sat a young woman in a long leather coat with an expensive fur collar. She smoked heavily, the pack of cigarettes set on the table in front of her. Her legs were crossed, the left firm on the ground while the right showed her tense, nervous state. Suddenly, she left her seat and moved toward the telephone in reception. She was still very nervous when she came back and started smoking once more.

The silence was broken by the sound of a raven landing on a bough outside our inn. As the raven croaked, I could see the breath from its beak and the flakes of snow shaken from the branch. It left me wondering about this strange bird that could exist in the hottest and coldest countries alike. God must, I reflected, have created such an ugly creature to help contrive some balance between beauty and ugliness. I felt a sense of unease. Here I was, in a room with an old person snoring, another person jittery and a raven croaking outside in the freezing snow. What a trip, I thought to myself!

A number of small birds had gathered now, on a leafless branch. Their wings, frozen, appeared as though made of crystal. At that moment a helicopter flew over the lake, dropping yellow and red balloons printed with the picture of the Loch Ness monster—an attempt to liven things up for the snowed-in tourists. Hitting the surface of the frozen lake, the balloons bounced off in all directions: a splendid sight, bringing with it feelings of contentment and a sense of freedom. Nothing, though, could distract me for long from this nervous woman, who had the air of a cat trapped in a cage. The telephone was the sole communication between the inn and the rest of the world; having that cut would have meant total isolation. The snow seemed to build walls, barriers that blocked you off from contact with anyone. For the first time in my life, I felt as though I'd lost my two legs. I sat, drinking my coffee and watching the nervous woman. At last I managed to find a way of staying occupied, of keeping my mind off this enforced siege.

I found myself, once more, reflecting on this small, magical machine we call the telephone. How could I conceive of living, in circumstances like these, with no phone to connect me with my family? Without that wondrous device, the place would have been like a graveyard. What an invention it was! It hadn't, surely, been contrived by someone whose brain was frozen the way that lake was; and nor, needless to say, had it been a brain like the brains of us desert people. Ours seemed to have melted from the heat—no wonder we'd never managed to come up with any useful invention. The one thing we invented with certainty was the hollow, empty language we call writing, which was akin to the raven's croaking.

Those living in cold countries had the creative brains: the ones that invented and made possible all we saw around us today. The truth was, we were like those ravens, a species good for nothing. You couldn't eat its meat, or keep it, or even make use of its feathers.

The theory needed more reflection. But who knows, maybe they'd studied these things already. Perhaps the results were stored somewhere on their computers, in one of their universities. And as usual no one had told us of the results.

We never wanted to learn anything. We couldn't even stir ourselves to begin learning anything. Learning scared us, just like the snowy vista that filled my heart with fear and loneliness. But was I just over-reacting, dishonoring my whole nation in the process? Was it maybe some kind of masochism or flight from reality?

She was standing by the window now, fiddling with her hair and smoking. She asked for a cup of coffee and took evident pleasure in drinking it very hot. The steam from the coffee, mixed with the smoke from her cigarette, thickened an atmosphere warm despite the falling snow.

What, I wondered, was wrong with this woman? What could have caused her such agitation and distress? You might have thought the snow outside could calm an active volcano!

I used, when I was younger, to be an inquisitive kind of person. Boldness, I thought, was a weapon harmless enough. Growing up, and facing life's problems, had rid me of the habit, but now here it suddenly was, back alive and kicking. I felt the driving urge, near impossible to curb, to find out this woman's secret. My old habit, not dead at all, must have woken from its slumber like a wolf answering the call of the wild.

A small table beside the bookshelves was the only thing between me and the woman. On the table were a stuffed bird and some dried wheat stalks; on the shelves various other items, like a stuffed squirrel and some old books I didn't bother to look at closely. I was focused on the woman. I went and stood alongside her. Would she mind, I asked, if I sat down? She looked at me in surprise, but said nothing. Giving her no chance to accept my presence or reject it, I grabbed a chair and pulled it to where she was sitting. I could smell the perfume she was wearing. She looked astonished now. For all the vague smile telling of her anger and distress, I sensed her mingled feelings, of disapproval, incredulity and annoyance, at what I'd done.

Apologizing for my intrusion, I told her I too was anxious at being trapped by the snow, here in this wretched place, and that I couldn't help noticing how very tense and upset she was. I was, I explained, a very sensitive kind of person, easily affected by my surroundings, and for that reason I'd been disturbed at the state she was in. In a place like this, I told her, remote and isolated, people were bound to feel a bond of compassion with one another.

"I'm sad, quite simply," I went on, "at the obvious distress you're in. I'd like to cheer you up if only I can, even if it means playing the fool."

She relaxed gradually, seeming to feel better. Perhaps she was wondering at this strange person, who was expressing such fine, cultivated feelings! As she became calmer, her anger seemed to grow more intense. The warmth surged out from her eyes, as spring water surges up from the earth. Her tension was melting away, like snow on a bough in springtime.

I felt a sense of exhilaration; not because I'd managed to tame this wild mare, but because I'd gambled and won. To her surprise, I ordered her a cup of coffee, which she drank as she listened to me.

"I should apologize," I said. "I haven't introduced myself properly. But as things are here, we surely don't need introductions with names—they just stop us getting lost in this wild world of ours—but with decent actions and feelings."

Her eyes open wide, she reached for her cigarettes and offered me one. I didn't smoke, I told her, although the sight of smoking chimneys made me feel warm and safe on cold nights. I sensed, from the language of her body, that she was making an attempt to get to know me better.

At this point we were interrupted by a hotel employee, who told her there was a problem of some kind with her credit card. She was horrified, and agitated too. "What am I going to do?" she exclaimed. She repeated the question, in a trembling voice, then fell back into her chair. I drew closer.

"What's the matter?" I asked. "Tell me, please."

She gazed at me sadly.

"It's all very complicated," she answered, "and I don't think there's anything you can do to help. For some reason my credit card isn't being accepted. The bank's closed for the holidays, and my friend's number isn't answering. I have a place booked to get back home, and I've asked for a special car to come and pick me up and take me to the train station. If I don't travel at the fixed time, I could lose my ticket, and my job as well. I have to pay for the fifteen days I've spent in this hotel. Do you understand now just what a problem I'm facing? I told you it was bigger than you could dream of!"

With that she burst into tears. I left her for a while, then returned with two cups of coffee. I tried to make her feel better, insisting she drank the coffee. The moment, though, that the hotel employee approached, her jittery manner returned. As he assured her she'd be able to travel as arranged, she stared at him in shocked disbelief. The employee then told her I'd taken care of the whole matter.

She looked at me as though I were "Nessie" just emerged from the lake.

"Don't worry," I told her, before she could say anything. "Perhaps we'll meet again some day. Or maybe not. It doesn't matter. I had enough money to help you out of your fix. It's all much easier than you might think. Money isn't worth more than the blood that keeps us alive."

She was still staring at me in disbelief, as I flashed her a smile that had all the warmth of the eastern sun, shining on their icy hills.

Um Rajoum

As the vehicle drove off along the sandy road, into the dark heart of the night, he sat listening to the squealing sounds it made at every turn and bump. He could hear the sound of the brakes each time they were used, and the shifting of the gears, as the vehicle drove on, filling the air and the passenger section with exhaust fumes. But now, as the way grew easier, they were speeding up, and the roar of the engine was gone.

The passengers were silent at first, thinking perhaps of their children and wives and families, and the lives they were leaving behind them. After half an hour, though, some of them began talking, while others started singing, urging the rest to join in. Others simply made themselves comfortable on their baggage and fell asleep.

A smell of cigarette smoke was coming from the driver's section, to the annoyance of one of the passengers.

"Almighty God!" he said. "Does the driver have to smoke?"

Another was about to bang on the glass partition, but a third stopped him.

"We're travellers," he said, "not public guardians. Anyway, he isn't smoking in our faces, is he?"

Um Rajoum

Yet another said they should just leave the driver alone, and the issue was finally dropped when two of the passengers started singing *Al-Hygeny* in such a delightful voice that a couple more joined in. The atmosphere grew peaceful, serene, as the singing went on, mingling with the sound of the engine and leaving the passengers suddenly homesick. They sat reminiscing on the old days, and on their youth and the happy times they'd left behind in their beloved village.

After three hours some scattered lights appeared, and one of the passengers said: "That's Wakrah." The noise of the vehicle changed once more, as it slowed down over the sandy track with all its trees and curves. Then they reached a road that was much harder, and full of bumps that made the vehicle rattle and shake. The driver came to a halt.

"We're making a short stop here," he said. "You can get out if you want to."

A lot of the passengers took him up, as a smell of gasoline filled the air and the hot engine started making cracking sounds. It was a cold night with a full moon, and the village was clearly visible there amid the vast desert. Not that it was really a village—just a few simple houses to the right of the road, dark, the people asleep inside. Some way from the houses was a stopping point with a small grocery store and a yard full of gasoline barrels, surrounded by old tires and piles of carefully stacked logs. There was a dog lying there, and a cat leaping to try and catch some of the grasshoppers clustered around the light.

In the yard were five wooden beds covered with palm leaves. The driver and his assistant sat down on one of these and asked for some tea and a *nargila*[10], while three of the passengers sat on another and ordered some tea too. The rest scattered around the vehicle, some simply lying down on the ground while others took a walk.

"We're going to be late, I reckon," an elderly passenger said. "The call to morning prayer isn't that far off, and we still haven't made a move."

No one bothered to answer him, and he climbed back in the vehicle, muttering irritably. The assistant, though, called out:

"Everyone back on board. Time to go!"

At that moment a blind man, with a woman guiding him, approached the vehicle, and the assistant told the passengers:

"Make some room for this old man and his wife."

The vehicle was already crowded, and the passengers didn't appear best pleased. No one, though, said anything. With a great deal of difficulty the blind man seated himself.

"There is no God but Almighty God," he said. "From the way you people are acting, you'd think I was sitting on your heads!"

No one said a word in reply. The vehicle resumed its journey through the desert amid total silence. All that could be heard was the sound of the vehicle at every bump and turn of the road. Everyone slept now. Some began snoring, while others even spoke a few words in their sleep. The first half of the night passed, the vehicle still piercing the darkness and silence of the desert, leaving just a trail of white dust behind it.

One of the passengers woke, yawned, looked at his watch, then went back to sleep. Some time later he woke once more and looked at his watch again. Worried now, he woke the passenger next to him.

"It's five hours since we left the village," he said. "And we still haven't reached Um Rajoum." Um Rajoum was a stopping point half way to the city. "We must be lost!"

Other passengers, hearing what he said, woke up. Very soon they were all awake, and the questions were flying. One of them knocked on the driver's section, and the driver looked back over his shoulder.

"What's the matter?" he said.

No one dared answer. The driver repeated his question.

"Are you sure," one of them asked finally, "we're going the right way?"

The driver stopped the vehicle and turned to look at the passengers.

"What fool," he said, "asked that question?"

No one ventured a reply. He cursed and spat, then finally returned to the wheel and drove on. At last, one of the passengers, growing restless, said:

"Hey, I think we *are* lost."

Two or three passengers felt he was right. But still the vehicle moved on. The men, restless and nervous now, were too frightened to say a word.

At last the same passenger shouted out again:

"We're lost. I swear to God we are! Why don't you all do something? Stop the driver! Do you want to die of thirst and get eaten by vultures and scavenging animals?"

The man kept shouting, amid a general hubbub. Finally one passenger banged on the driver's section. The vehicle stopped. The driver got out and looked at the passenger.

"We're lost," the man yelled again. "With all the distance we've gone, we should be there by now."

The driver, saying nothing, just looked around and rubbed his hands. The passengers got out, gazing up at the sky in terror and despair. They'd lost all sense of direction—some of them couldn't even make out where earth and sky met. They were hardly to blame; it was known well enough how the desert could simply swallow up those who were lost, leaving them, within days, as gleaming skeletons.

The driver sat and began drawing heavily on his cigarette. No one was afraid of him any more. The passenger who'd first realized they were lost told him he might at least have saved some gasoline, if he'd only listened to them from the start.

"It's our fault," another said. "We should never have trusted this useless driver."

At that, one young man leaped at the driver, ready to hit him, but the others held him back.

"I was going to get married," he yelled, still spitting and shouting at the driver. "My wedding was next Thursday. And now I'm going to die before it can happen. Let me kill this bastard!"

Soon, though, everyone calmed down and accepted the facts of the situation. The young man was crying bitterly now and being comforted by the elderly passenger.

"Trust in God, my son," the old man told him, taking his hand. "Don't kill yourself with despair. If you're destined to live, nothing can kill you."

The desperate passengers spread themselves around the vehicle. Some lay down on the ground, some walked around in circles, while others prayed. The blind man and his wife, who'd been sitting together, now began to walk around, the blind man touching the scrubby bushes and the stones and sand. He'd do this for a time, take a rest, then start all over again. Finally, guided by his wife, he returned carrying pieces of the bushes he'd found and told the other passengers to gather around him.

"Do you know where we are?" he asked.

Some thought they were heading south, others said east, while still others were adamant they'd been driving west.

Next he told them to look at the moon. They did so, but couldn't say in which direction it was. The blind man laughed.

"Where are your shadows?" he asked.

Their shadows, they told him, were opposite to where the moon was.

"The moon moves west," he told them. "Now we just have to decide whether we're heading north or south."

He told them to help him stand facing the moon.

"Can you see," he said, "a star to my right, and above it two other stars, one shining very bright, the other not so bright? And then, above all those, seven stars, four of them in a group?"

They stood gazing up at the stars. They said they could, first hesitantly, then with more certainty. At that the blind man walked to the vehicle and said:

"We're heading south."

Then, turning to the driver, he asked:

"How much gasoline do we have left?"

"A quarter of a tank," the driver said.

The blind man looked alarmed.

"Listen," he said. "We're in a district called al-Hadbaa. I recognize it from the bushes and stones, and the smell of the sand. There are no villages around here, and no springs. Anyone who gets lost here is bound to die, and we're close to death ourselves. But we must trust in God. This isn't the time or place for blaming one another, or for weeping and wailing. We're four hours' drive from Um Rajoum, and the gasoline's barely enough for the trip. We must act quickly and leave before sunrise."

Then, turning to the driver, he said:

"Follow the moon and tell me the moment it disappears."

And so they began their journey, engulfed by the night, plunged in utter silence, and in fear and prayer. Now they drove quickly, now slowly. At each moment hope was born, only to be smothered by despair once more. There was no light, not a single camel, no living creature of any kind. Little by little the moon disappeared, till they were left in pitch darkness. The driver said:

"The moon's gone."

"You remember the goat star?" the driver said. "The one I showed you back there? Drive on, keeping it to your right."

"We haven't an hour's gasoline left," the driver said. "One mistake and we're all dead."

The passengers, anxious and frightened, began to wonder if they'd been right, leaving their fate in the hands of a blind man. But the blind man just retorted:

"It's your fault we got lost in the first place. Do you want us to die because of you?"

"Do as he tells you," the elderly passenger shouted, "and have faith in God!"

The night felt long indeed, and so did the road, as they drove on. After an hour had passed, and still they could see nothing, despair began to creep in. Suddenly the red light came on.

"We're out of gasoline, blind man," the driver said. "We're going to die, here in the middle of nowhere." With that the vehicle jerked and came to a halt.

"You've done for us," the passengers yelled, "you blind old fool!"

They got out of the vehicle, sat down and started to weep, waiting for the end they knew was coming. Their faces were pale, death written all over them. Nothing could be heard, in the silence, but their heavy breathing and the pounding of their hearts in their breasts.

They'd entered the valley of death; nothing,

not even the coming dawn, could bring hope to their hearts. When the sun did rise at last, they wouldn't, they knew, live to see it set, and fear took hold of them in earnest. They lay down, as if making ready to welcome death. It was as though, bent on doing away with themselves, they'd all taken some poison. Nothing was left but silence—the silence of a world with no existence.

Then the blind man's wife cried out, as though hit by a thunderbolt. No one bothered to look at her. Once more she cried out: "It's all right! It's all right!" She walked about among them now, pointing. "Look!" she shouted. "Over there!"

There at last, far off in the early morning light, Um Rajoum had appeared.

Notes

ABU RASHEED

[1] *Um*: Mother. Women in many Arab countries are commonly called "Um" followed by the name of their first-born child (but with the male having precedence over the female even if younger). The male equivalent is "Abu," seen throughout this story.

[2] *Bisht*: Outer garment worn over the other clothes (also called *abaya*).

[3] *Salamat:* A formula used, in this case, to imply relief after a mishap (i.e. that something more serious has not happened).

THE COMPOSITION LESSON

[4] *Igal*: Headband used to keep in place the traditional long Arab headgear, or *ghutra*.

[5] *Ghutra*: See note 4 above.

THE TUNNEL

[6] A famous line of Arabic poetry.

THE COMMITTEE

[7] Al-Jahiz (born c. 776, died 868 or 869): theologian, intellectual and a major and versatile writer, whose work was marked by a strong vein of humor. His *Book of Animals* was a bestiary anthologizing and commenting on Arabic writings and anecdotes with animal themes.

[8] Tawfiq al-Hakim: Major twentieth-century Egyptian writer who was strongly instrumental in modernizing Arabic drama. His celebrated book *My Donkey Told Me* was a humorous commentary on life.

FLOCKS OF DOVES

[9] These are all characters who, like the subject of the story, were consumed by longing. Maysoun, wife of the Umayyad caliph Muawiyah, was constantly wretched away from the desert to which she was eventually permitted to return. Fatima is the person referred to at the beginning of the story, lover of the poet al-Murraqqash in pre-Islamic Yemen. Waddah al-Yaman, a romantic poet of the Umayyad period, suffered from his impossible love for a lady of noble status.

UM RAJAM

[10] *Nargila*: A kind of pipe in which the tobacco is drawn through water.